TORCHWOOD

# THE HOUSE THAT
# JACK BUILT

T0315599

Recent titles in the *Torchwood* series from BBC Books:

# TORCHWOOD
## THE HOUSE THAT JACK BUILT

Guy Adams

BBC BOOKS

6 8 10 9 7 5

Published in hardback in 2009 by BBC Books, an imprint of Ebury Publishing.
A Random House Group company.
This paperback edition published in 2012.

Torchwood is a BBC Wales production for BBC One. Executive Producers: Russell T
Davies and Julie Gardner. Original series created by Russell T Davies and broadcast on
BBC Television. 'Torchwood' and the Torchwood logo are trademarks of the
British Broadcasting Corporation and are used under licence.

The Random House Group Limited Reg. No. 954009. Addresses for companies within
the Random House Group can be found at www.randomhouse.co.uk

A CIP catalogue record for this book is available from the British Library.

ISBN 978 1 849 90607 4

Penguin Random House is committed to a sustainable future for
our business, our readers and our planet. This book is made from
Forest Stewardship Council® certified paper.

MIX
Paper | Supporting
responsible forestry
FSC® C018179

Printed and bound in Great Britain by Clays Ltd, St Ives plc

Commissioning Editor: Albert DePetrillo
Series Editor: Steve Tribe
Production: Alex Goddard
Cover design by Lee Binding © Woodlands Books Ltd 2009

*To my wonderful Debra,*
*who always reassures me I can write*
*when I'm quite convinced I can't.*

Nothing seemed more important to Danny Wilkinson that afternoon than the spikiness of his fringe. He wanted it to *loom*. Doused in Hugo Boss aftershave (stolen from his older brother), he hoped the two bent – but smokable – fags in his back pocket would be the clincher, the carrot at the end of a stick that might lure Amy Woodyatt's lips onto his. Play his cards right and he might even get the top of her jeans loose enough for a little investigation.

Penylan didn't look as if it shared his enthusiasm, cold and austere, the architectural embodiment of 'don't do this' and 'don't do that'. The Edwardian terraces looked disapprovingly down their gables at him as he crossed towards Roath Park. Perhaps they knew who he was meeting; certainly his parents didn't or they would never have let him out of the house. Josh Biggs was on every Penylan parent's 'forbidden list' after being caught selling weed in the playground of St Teilo's a couple of weeks back.

A chill breeze pulled its way through the remaining leaves on the trees. Danny kicked a pebble along the surface of the road, scuffing his soles in the grit and dancing with the pretend football. He flicked it up and belted it hard, dreaming of roaring stadium terraces. The pebble flew, clipping a few stray privet leaves from a garden hedge before knocking its way through the streaked glass of the window behind it.

'Bollocks…' Danny whispered, about to run until he realised the house was empty. Nobody had lived at Jackson Leaves for months. He and Josh had watched an ambulance crew carry an old woman out of its front door ages ago. They had noted every detail: the blue-veined milk of her loose skin, the faint condensation on the inside of the oxygen mask. Death about to happen. He doubted she was in a position to care about her window any more.

This street held only big, detached houses, all set back from the road with the sort of private parking area rich mothers left luxurious four-by-fours on. Jackson Leaves was letting the side down though, being long past its presentable best. The hedge was overgrown, the gravel forecourt peppered with weeds, jagged dandelion leaves and creeping thistles. Cobwebs fluttered like curtains from the wooden eaves. The windows were dirty, as blind as the old woman had seemed when lifted into the back of the ambulance.

Danny stared at it from across the street, taking a small amount of pride in the black bullet hole the pebble had left in the front, downstairs window. Not a bad shot… not a bad shot at all. Somewhere a radio was playing loud, jolly rhythms, trying to convince the streets towards cheerfulness and failing.

Heading towards the park, he fell as his foot was suddenly yanked out from underneath him. He got his hands up in time to stop his chin colliding with the tarmac but gave a shout of pain as he felt loose grit cut into his palms.

Carefully pushing himself up, he gave another cry as his right hand burst through the surface of the pavement, vanishing up to the elbow.

The ground beneath him bubbled, the surface of the pavement gripping the toes of his trainers as if the tarmac were freshly poured. He pulled at his trapped hand, but the pavement clung to him like syrup. Stuck on all fours, he began to sink.

His mum had told him the story of *Br'er Rabbit and the Tar-Baby* when he was little. He had been terrified, picturing the glistening man made of tar that Br'er Rabbit had fought, the animal becoming more and more glued to his opponent with every blow. It had given him nightmares for weeks, dreams of a hot, black embrace and steaming mouths lowering down onto his…

He shouted for help, tipping his head back and bellowing even as the tarmac gave up all pretence of solidity and sucked him straight down. The shout was cut off in his throat as the ground suddenly hardened again, his teeth slamming onto solid pavement in splinters of enamel. He couldn't cry out at the pain, the earth and rubble in his throat choked all hope of that. Nothing could get past it, most certainly not air.

It took him longer than he might have liked to die.

# ONE

'What do *you* think? Green or pink?'

Rhys realised Gwen was talking and, more than that, she had asked an important question that he had no idea how to answer. 'The first one,' he gambled, 'it's much more…' And there he ran out of steam. '… *Nice*,' he tried.

'Fat lot of use you are.'

Gwen smiled. H&M was like Kryptonite to Rhys; he'd slip into a coma if forced to stand outside its changing rooms for more than five minutes. 'Why don't you go and look at DVDs next door?' she suggested. 'If you hang around here any longer you'll probably die of boredom.'

'I don't mind,' Rhys replied, trying not to stare at the posters of the underwear models.

Gwen pushed him gently towards the exit.

'I'll survive on my own. Go on.'

'Aye, right.' He gave her a peck on the cheek and headed towards the exit, throwing the occasional worried glance at clothing as he passed, as if concerned it might bite him. He passed a pregnant woman laden down with clothes and found himself imagining Gwen with a similar bulge. He smiled. Most of his mates had predictable fantasies about their partners in kinky underwear or lesbian trysts; he pictured Gwen the size of a house and cursing his name as she went in to labour. He was a soppy sod sometimes.

Gwen walked back into the changing room, tugging the green top to get it to sit right. Spotting the pregnant lady's reflection shuffle its way into one of the changing cubicles behind her, her response was a world away from Rhys's, remembering the arguments she'd had with him on the subject. Torchwood and breeding just weren't the best of bedfellows. Not that she would be so opposed to it otherwise – she could easily see herself bringing up a child with Rhys, he'd make an excellent father. Still, balancing a life of babies and alien invasions? No… no thanks.

The pregnant woman grunted and an elbow ballooned the cubicle curtain as she struggled to move in the confined space. A blouse fell to the floor by the woman's feet. Nice, Gwen thought, very fitted… Sexy.

*Fitted.*

The woman bent over, grabbed the blouse and stood back up. There was the sound of more struggling before she suddenly yanked back the curtain and stormed out, looking for all the world as if she'd lost her temper and given up on the idea of clothes shopping. Gwen didn't believe it for a moment. She was still wondering why a pregnant woman would take a blouse into the changing room that she could never possibly wear.

She ran out of the changing room and onto the shop floor, chasing after the woman's retreating head and shoulders. She was making straight for the exit.

'Oi!' One of the girls behind the till shouted as Gwen left the shop and ran into the arcade. The woman she was chasing turned around on hearing the shout, and the look on her face was more than enough to convince Gwen that her instinct had been right. She launched herself at her, the pair of them hitting the floor with shoppers panicking around them.

'Bloody hell!' she heard someone shout. 'Get the mad bitch off her!'

Oh yeah, jumping on pregnant women… not a crowd pleaser that. She made a grab for the woman's bloated belly as hands gripped her by the shoulders. There was the tearing of fabric, and a bundle of carefully wrapped clothes spilled onto the floor. The woman's pregnant belly was a tightly stuffed pouch of stolen clothes.

'Now if I'd done that the papers would have been giving my knackers away as a Sunday supplement.' Gwen smiled when she saw who had grabbed her: her old police partner Andy Davidson.

'Fancy seeing you here,' said Gwen.

'Someone reported a mad cow on the rampage in Boots, spraying people with baby oil. Not you by any chance?'

'I have an alibi.'

'Oh yes, where is Rhys? Scoffing a few pasties?'

'Don't be mean.'

'Just my way. You know I love him really.'

He lifted his handcuffs off his belt and put them on the shoplifter's wrists.

'I was going to give you a bell, actually,' he continued, his attention back on Gwen. 'Just had a call through about something spooky in Penylan. Sounded right up your street.'

'Oh yeah?' Gwen wasn't sure she liked the sound of that.

'Aye, some kid found embedded in a pavement, you know, like literally *embedded*…'

'Come on, Andy.' Gwen gave a pointed look at the shoplifter. 'Time and a place, eh?'

'Oh… yeah… well, y'know… if you're not interested?'

Gwen sighed and reached for her mobile.

'But do I really need the poker chips and playing cards?' Rhys wondered aloud. 'I mean, special features are good, yeah, but games compendiums? Seems a waste of money. They'll be putting *Cluedo* in with *Poirot* next.'

The shop assistant was new and still had some enthusiasm for the job and an urge to make sales. 'The poker stuff's just a bonus,' he said. 'It's the first twenty-one Bond movies in two-disc, digitally remastered editions…'

'"Digitally remastered", is it?' Rhys scoffed. 'It's a wonder we ever managed to watch the crappy old things really.' His mobile rang and, seeing Gwen's name on the screen, he looked around as if he'd been caught in a drug transaction. 'All right, love, won't be long, will I? I'll have a cappu- oh… You what? … Bloody hell, Gwen! I only turn my back for five minutes and there's a national emergency is there? … No… No… I know you can't… No… Right.'

He ended the call, shoving the phone back in his jeans with a sigh.

'Twenty-one films, is it?' he said to the shop assistant. 'That's a lot of hours filled. I'll take it.'

There's nothing quite like the luxury of a cup of coffee prepared by *someone else*. The sort of coffee that you watch someone labour over. You watch them grind the beans, fill the scoop, steam the milk, pump the espresso. Then, if you're Ianto Jones, you watch them pick you out a juicy Pain au Raisin and drop that fruity bad boy into a takeaway bag. *Nice*.

Having found a *barista* whose coffee-making skill he actually trusted, Ianto was becoming quite the fan of having someone else do all the work. The fact that this Queen of the Beans, this Empress of the Roast, was a grumpy little Chinese girl whose service was lousy and attitude abominable didn't take the edge off it in the least.

She could spit in his eye if she so wished. As long as she didn't do it in his coffee, he would pay her with a smile.

He didn't sip at his cappuccino as he walked along the jetty to the Tourist Information entrance, preferring to wait and drink it with his pastry, his own perfect little moment. Having had the first good run of sleep in about a week – the fact that it had taken place during the day being neither here nor there; when part of Torchwood, you grabbed it when you found it – he was determined to continue his good fortune over a nice relaxing breakfast. Or afternoon tea, he thought, checking his watch with a sigh.

He unlocked the Tourist Information door, stepped inside and locked it again behind him. The grockles were not well served on the Marina of late. He'd opened for maybe two days over the last fortnight, things having been just too busy for maintaining the cover. Reaching over the counter, he tapped in the four-digit code sequence that opened the concealed door in the wall. Saluting a rather tatty poster of Max Boyce with his coffee cup, Ianto stepped into the tunnels beyond, cutting through their damp gloominess with a whistle. Even the distant scuttle of rats couldn't intrude on his good mood.

At the main gate, the entry code was long enough to feel like a piano piece as he beat it out on the lock-pad. The heavy door rolled out of the way and finally he was in.

'Hello?' he shouted. No reply. *Perfect.* He was on his own.

He settled at his desk and booted up the RSS reader. Popping the white cap off his coffee, he grabbed the pastry bag and settled back in his chair with a sigh. The rest of the day could not go wrong, not from such sturdy foundations, it was *unthinkable*.

While scrolling through BBC News with one hand, he brought up the sensor reports for the hours he'd been away. Torchwood had Cardiff wired up like a politician in a hooker's boudoir: there wasn't a mouse fart that was not catalogued and calibrated by one sensor or another. You had to be attentive when you had a space-time event outside your window, it moved things around while you slept.

He took a bite of his pastry, a stray raisin tumbling over his bottom lip and skydiving into his lap. He tutted and flicked it away. Reaching for the serviette that came in the bag, he tucked it above his perfectly knotted tie – full Windsor, naturally – like a bib. He didn't altogether care what the pastry did to his waistline, but it could keep its damned paws off his suit.

His attention was drawn by a chronon spike in the Penylan area. It didn't have the temporal decay signature of the Rift, but he couldn't think what else it might be. He entered Penylan as a search filter for police radio traffic. The two seconds it took to offer the fate of Danny Wilkinson to his screen was more than enough time for a mouthful of pastry, but after reading the transcript he didn't fancy another.

\*\*\*

The oak tree sagged pitifully in the centre of the recreational lawn. When it shuffled its leaves in the wind it was with the bored resignation of an underpaid conjuror, struggling his way through a card trick at a particularly awful children's party. The attitude was contagious: *nobody* carried themselves with enthusiasm at the Mercy Hill Care Home. The residents could be excused – enthusiasm, like a solid bowel movement, was ancient history to most of them – but even the staff sighed their way through the day, gazing listlessly into the middle distance as if waiting for death. It was not a cheerful place, and that reason alone was sufficient cause for Alexander – a congenitally miserable bastard – to make it his home.

He sat beneath the dejected oak and watched as various residents pottered their way around the garden. He tutted at Trudy Topham, standing in the middle of a rhododendron bush, spilling fragile memories into the breeze from her slack mouth. Someone would fetch her back inside just as soon as they could be bothered. In the distance, Leon Harris could be seen making one of his twice-weekly bids for freedom. Staff usually caught up with him before he made it past the fence, but every once in a while he managed a little further. He had once been found crawling along the central reservation of the M4, but that was a few years ago now and his legs were no longer as strong as they were. Alexander stretched back in his wheelchair, yawning and playing on the bony xylophone of his ribs with his fingers.

'Careful now, Mr Martin,' Nurse Sellers said in his ear. 'We don't want you falling out, do we?'

Alexander was half-tempted to try, if only so he could cop a feel of her weighty breasts on his chin while she manhandled him back into his chair. Reduced to pratfalls in order to arouse oneself… there were times when he absolutely despaired. He sank back into his chair with a sigh.

'No, nurse, we don't. Any sign of this doctor of yours yet?'

'He's no doctor of *ours*, Mr Martin,' Nurse Sellers stressed, as if to a particularly slow child. 'I did explain that. He's sent by the Council to judge our standards.'

'Worried?'

'Don't be silly… I'll thank you not to suggest you've received anything but the very best of care here at Mercy Hill.'

'Wouldn't dream of it.' He gave a brief smile. 'Cross my heart and hope for a cardiac team on standby. So who do you think ratted you out?'

'It is not a question of being "ratted out", as you put it, Mr Martin. All care homes receive independent visits from time to time. You're just lucky that it was your name he picked out of his hat.'

'Aren't I just? The thrill is almost sexual.'

'No need for that sort of talk, Mr Martin.'

'No,' said Alexander, trying to see the line of her underwear through her uniform. 'Quite right.'

'Here he comes now.'

'Good morning, Alexander!' said the man walking across the lawn towards them. Alexander felt a momentary panic as he recognised the face (if not the white coat and casually dangled stethoscope). It took a second for a name to drop alongside that horribly perfect smile. Harkness... yes, that was it. Captain Jack Harkness. 'Morning to you too, of course, nurse,' Jack added, offering a small bow towards her. 'A beauty powerful enough to cure any ill.'

Nurse Sellers chuckled like a schoolgirl. Alexander rolled his eyes.

'You're too kind, doctor,' she replied. 'If only you were a regular visitor to our humble home.'

Jack stepped in close and smiled. 'Maybe you'll get to see a bit more of me down the line,' he winked.

Alexander sighed. 'If you don't mind?' he said. 'I believe he's here to see me.'

Nurse Sellers gave him a scathing look, not taking kindly to having her fun spoiled. 'Well, his time's precious, I'm sure,' she said. 'I know *I* wouldn't want to waste any of it.'

The inference that he *was* wasn't lost on Alexander, but Jack rescued the situation before it could descend into further argument. 'You're quite right, I have got a lot on today. Better give the old goat his onceover, eh?'

She smiled and strode towards the main house, her hips swinging so much it was a wonder she didn't snap her pelvis.

'Old goat?' Alexander sighed. 'Cheeky bugger.'

'You're just jealous,' Jack said, leaning against the tree. 'You'd love to whisk her away on your wheelchair and do unforgivable things to her in the bushes.'

Alexander refused to rise to this, not least because there was a degree of truth in it. Safest plan by far was just to change the subject. 'I thought I'd end up bumping into you sooner or later. When was it we last…?'

'Crossed paths?' Jack replied. 'Relative time's a nightmare. It was years ago for me… The Spice Bazaar on Velecerol. You were pretending to be some sort of health inspector, or was it customs official?'

'The customs official was on Balthazar. I impounded your ship, if you remember.'

Jack chuckled. 'That's right. You always did tend to bite off more than you could chew.'

'Nonsense.' Alexander reclined in his wheelchair and gazed up at the wafting leaves of the tree. 'I simply decided to let you have it back. It didn't suit my purposes…'

'Lucky me.'

'How did you know I was here? I was fairly certain I'd covered my tracks.'

'Pure luck…' Jack removed a small device from the pocket of his white coat, like a TV remote control but flatter. 'Spotted you at the hospital the other day.'

'Oh yes…' Alexander sighed. 'I can see how rampaging hordes of the living dead might have drawn Torchwood's attention rather.' He glanced towards Jack. 'Despite that lovely coat, you are working for Torchwood now, I believe?'

'Working for? Not quite… I'm *running* things here in Cardiff.'

'You always were an ambitious boy.' He pointed at the device in Jack's hand. 'What's that?'

Jack aimed the device at him, pressed a button and swept the sensor over Alexander's body. The machine beeped a couple of times as it processed the gathered information and he handed it over. 'I've got a job offer for you,' he said. 'This is the medical.'

Alexander scanned through the data Jack had captured. 'Core temperature twenty-four degrees, heart rate forty-six beats per minute… I'd say that was fine.'

'For a Kanatian. I hate to think what that nurse would make of these readings.'

'I have medication for that.' Alexander patted his pocket and there was the rattle of pills. 'If you'd swept that thing over me a minute or two later, my vital signs would have been within human norm. I took two before she wheeled me out here. I wasn't given much notice, otherwise I'd have taken them earlier. How do you think I've not been picked up by your lot sooner? Not all doctors are as untrained as you – excepting of course your no doubt encyclopaedic knowledge of genitalia.'

Jack smiled, unbundled the stethoscope from his pocket and huffed on the end of it. 'I have an excellent bedside manner at least.'

'You're mistaking patient interaction for pillow talk. What's the job offer?'

'I'm short a medical officer, wondered if you'd be

willing to step in, as a temporary fix.'

'Let me guess, more post-mortems than I can shove a thermometer up?'

'Pretty much.'

'Sounds charming, but I'm far too busy here watching these crumbling idiots skip towards the grave.'

Jack looked at Trudy, still muttering in the undergrowth. 'I can see the appeal.'

Alexander followed his gaze. 'Careful. She's lived in Cardiff all her life, she's probably an ex-girlfriend.'

'Not my type.'

'Mad as a hatter and likely to whip her nightie off at the least provocation, I would have thought she was your *only* type.'

'Bitch.'

'*Bastard*, if you don't mind. How am I supposed to keep getting out of this place to see to these dead bodies of yours?'

'You're a creative man, you'll manage. Either that or let me set you up an apartment in town. It's not like you need to be here.'

'I'm not good on my own.'

'Funny, I can never imagine you any other way. Are you going to take the job?'

'What's the pay?'

'Like you need money.'

'Everyone needs money. You can pay the bill on this place for a year, regardless of how long I'm on the books.'

'Done… Considering the service, I can't believe it's that expensive.'

'You'd be surprised. They wipe your arse every day whether you need it or not. That sort of residential care comes at a cost.'

'I'm sure the budget can handle it.'

'Good, in that case it can pay me a bonus: one good bottle of Single Malt per patient.'

'And have you drunk at the operating table?'

'Alcohol doesn't affect my species. I just like the taste.'

'Now I understand why you're always so miserable. Is there nothing Kanatians do for fun?'

'War was popular.'

A bleeping noise went off in Jack's pocket.

'Ah… the world needs saving.' Alexander smiled. 'Square jaw and hair gel, go get 'em, kid.'

'You might be right,' Jack said, noting Gwen's mobile on the pager.

'I usually am.' Alexander offered Jack a rare, genuine smile. 'You'll shout if you need me?'

Jack reached into his other pocket and handed Alexander a pager identical to his own. 'On this.'

Alexander took it. 'Can't wait. Off you go then, fight the good fight.'

Jack gave Alexander a gentle squeeze on the shoulder. 'Want me to drop you off somewhere?' he asked, tapping the wheelchair handles.

'I'm perfectly capable, thank you.'

'More than anyone here would ever guess, I'm sure.'

'Quite. Now go away and leave me to the company of my peers.'

As Alexander spoke, Leon Harris was being dragged back from the neighbouring field, his language proving that crudity was not the sole province of the young.

# TWO

Julia held Rob's hand and tried not feel as if she had let her aunt down. When you see your dentist more often than your family, it's hard to avoid a little guilt when they die. There were just the two of them in the church, an old man sat in the front row having left with a curse as he realised 'his old mate Len' wasn't due for cremation until later on that afternoon.

The vicar – a thin, red-faced man who stumbled behind his lectern like a drunken Swan Vesta – did his best not to let the false start faze him as he launched into his prepared speech extolling the virtues of the deceased. Perhaps the virtues were accurate. It was fuel to Julia's guilt that she hadn't known the woman well enough to be sure.

Aunt Joan had been a passing figure from childhood,

a slightly austere dispenser of the occasional sweet and two pounds at Christmas. Julia hadn't expected to inherit anything from her – or from *anyone* for that matter, she had never thought in such terms. She might not luxuriate in the flat she and Rob shared as snugly as the bank overdraft that went with it, but she was content with it. They had made it their home.

As the cheap theatrics proceeded, she had to admit this was no way to gain a house. There was a depressing clunk as the lift mechanism carried Aunt Joan towards the furnace and an escape from this terrible funeral and, indeed, from everything else. When the coffin vanished, Julia realised she had been holding her breath. She breathed out, her exhalation echoing around the chapel like an escaping spirit.

'That was painful,' Julia said to Rob in the snug of the Clement Bishop, just across the road from the crematorium.

He gave her shoulder a squeeze and took a sip of his Guinness, a drink dressed for a funeral. 'At least we were there for her,' he said, scratching at the stubble he always ended up wearing past dinner-time. The only thing Rob Wallace Painting Services couldn't make presentable was his own chin. 'It's depressing to think someone can go through life and not gather friends.'

'People lose touch.'

'Everyone?' He took another mouthful of his pint as if to wash the thought away.

Julia spun her wine glass around by its stem. The chilled white felt too vibrant on her subdued palate, like a scream in a library. 'Let's just go home,' she said as Rob's pint sank to a drainable level. 'We need to finish the packing.'

'Jackson Leaves' insisted the name-plaque that hung alongside the front door.

'Of course he does,' Julia said.

'Weird name,' Rob replied.

'Weird house.' She prodded the plaque with her thumb. It was screwed into the brick. 'We can live with it for now.'

She unlocked the door and they stepped into a hallway lined with black-and-white tiles and the musk of years.

Rob's eye was caught by an old photo just inside the door – an attractive young woman who reminded him of his wife, despite the lack of blonde hair. 'She has your looks,' he said, as Julia pushed the mountain of collected junk mail along the hall with her foot.

'I suppose it's more accurate to say I've got hers.'

In the sitting room, a collection of easy chairs sagged under the weight of cobwebs and dust that reclined on them.

'We could hold church meetings here,' Rob joked. 'You could bake cakes.'

Julia smacked the back of one of the chairs, stepping back as a mushroom cloud of dust threatened to envelop her. 'Old people collect abandoned function rooms like they do liver spots,' she said. 'Retreating through their homes until they end up hiding in one little room. Depressing.'

'Yep,' Rob agreed. 'The sooner we clear all this stuff out and make the place our own the better.' He caught an uncomfortable glance from Julia and was worried that he might have spoken out of turn. 'I don't mean we just junk *everything*. I mean it's your aunt's belongings, I understand if you want to—'

'Don't worry about it,' Julia interrupted, not wanting to see her husband tie himself in knots. 'None of it means a thing. I just…' Her voice trailed away, her thoughts as fragile as the strands of cobweb she'd snapped pacing across the room.

'It's big.'

Julia smiled. Some days, she and Rob seemed to share a mind. 'Isn't it? Three floors, God knows how many rooms… We filled the flat.'

'Plus some.'

'OK, it was snug but we fitted in it. We're just going to rattle here…' She stared at the gap between the stair banisters that took her eyes straight to the roof at the top. 'This place is hollow.'

'And worth a few quid once I've done it up.'

Julia nodded. She knew the rational arguments, had started most of them; she just wished she hadn't felt so small the minute she'd stepped through the front door.

Later, they sat and ate fish and chips out of the paper, the traditional dinner of new homes, kitchen crockery left in its packing crate for one more night.

'The work won't take long,' Rob said as he sent a thick chunk of cod diving into a sea of ketchup. 'I mean it depends how many other jobs crop up, but the phone doesn't ring itself silly most weeks, does it? Lick of paint, fire safety doors, then we can get some students in.'

Julia had abandoned her meal and scooted her paper across the lounge floorboards so that Rob could hoover up her leftover chips. 'Maybe we should start advertising the place straight away?'

Outside there was the rumbling of a storm.

'Let's just hope the roof doesn't leak,' she said, kissing her husband's greasy lips.


They were making love by the time the rain began to fall. The roof *didn't* leak, but Julia felt the storm was in the room with them nonetheless. If only she could shake this nervous feeling – there was no reason for it that she could think of. She had no bad memories of the house. In fact she had no strong memories of it at all. There was just something in the atmosphere, something she could *taste*.

Their lovemaking sputtered out with a conciliatory kiss from her distracted lips, and she lay back on the inflatable mattress that was their first-night bed. She made patterns from the shadows the rain cast in the amber of the streetlights. Her state of mind led her time and again to picture screaming faces, eager gallows, severed limbs. As sleep took her, she was desperate for the happy feelings that would let her see butterflies.

She woke later to the knowledge that they were not alone. She stared at the darkness that had settled in the far corner of the bedroom and strained to see straight lines and shapes in it. Just as she managed to identify a face, seemingly hovering in the air, it vanished, leaving her to question whether it had even been there in the first place.

With morning came an even greater desperation to dismiss her unease. She tried the noise of unpacking and the reassuring smell and hiss of fried bacon. Neither worked. Once the portable stereo was unpacked, she tried heavier artillery, turning up the radio volume so that the voices and songs were shouts of opinion and melody. It was so loud she failed to hear the sound of breaking glass from the cobweb-ridden front room when Danny Wilkinson sent a stray pebble through its window. In fact, a little later, she nearly missed a call from Rob as he rang her on the mobile.

'Open the door, would you?' he said. 'Forgotten my keys. What's going on anyway?'

'What do you mean?'

'Cordoned off the road, haven't they?'

She opened the front door to find the police just along from her front gate. Rob had parked the van several doors up, an inconvenience as the back was stuffed full of what little furniture they owned. He and his mate Steve were walking down the street, a mattress wobbling between them. Looking at the police tape, every disturbed feeling she'd had since the night before became real. She made eye contact with a dark-haired woman who was getting out of her car and heading towards the police tent. The woman gave what was meant to be a reassuring smile, but Julia wasn't so easily assuaged.

'What's happened?' she shouted, but the woman vanished beyond the police tape.

'Probably a gas leak or summat,' Steve said as he and Rob worked their way past her.

Rob rolled his eyes. 'Thanks for that. Big comfort, *really.*'

Julia ignored them as they vanished into the house. She walked down the path and tried to get a glimpse of whatever was going on. The policemen marched out, got in their cars and drove away. That had to be a good sign, surely?

Stepping into the street, her heart jumped into her mouth as a black four-by-four came speeding along the road towards her. The car pulled up sharply and a tall man jumped out.

'Sorry about that, didn't see you coming.'

He was handsome but his vintage military clothing made her suspect he would never be her 'type'.

'What's happened?' she asked, still the only question she had any interest in.

'Couldn't tell you,' he replied, his American accent as unusual in Cardiff suburbia as his clothing. 'I just got here. You too?'

She had to look over her own shoulder to understand what he meant. Rob and Steve were forcing the mattress through the front door. 'Oh… Yes, just moving in.'

'It's a nice house,' he sounded like he was reassuring her rather than passing comment. Whatever the intention, he had nothing else to say, turning his back on her and following the dark-haired woman beyond the police tape.

Julia stared after them for a while before moving back across the road and into her drive.

'The Wilkinson boy,' said a woman's voice from beyond the privet hedge that lined Jackson Leaves.

Julia peered through the foliage. The speaker was wreathed in cheap gold and cigarette smoke, mouthfuls of which she puffed onto the breeze as she worked her way through the length of a Dunhill.

'Dead as you like, buried in the pavement.'

'I'm sorry?' Julia felt as if she were still making dream shapes from the silhouettes of rain. Nothing was making sense.

'Kid from up the way. Buried in the ground, he was, arms and legs sticking out all over.'

'That's horrible.'

'It is, and you can bet there'll be drugs behind it. They're *all* on drugs these days.'

Later, Rob and Steve were putting flat-pack furniture together as if everything was all right.

Maybe it was. Julia found she still couldn't tell. She

watched from the dirty (and now broken) front window as the police tape, tent and investigators vanished and rain appeared. There was a big trench by the side of the road where a chunk of the pavement had been removed – she could see it filling with water. She tried to imagine what the body might have looked like.

'Don't suppose you could make us a cup of tea, could you?' Rob asked from behind her. 'That bed frame's turning out to be a right bastard, and Steve's moaning about the lack of service.' He shifted awkwardly in the doorway. 'You know what he's like… *gobby*.'

Julia nodded and made her way through to the kitchen. She should get on anyway, staring out of the window wasn't going to make her feel any better. She needed to crack on, knock the unfamiliar away and start making this home. As she worked her way through the last of the kitchen things, she almost felt normal, even convinced herself that there wasn't the faint outline of a fat man watching her from the back garden, that it was nothing but the rain.

# THREE

Gwen pulled up alongside the cordoned-off police tent that was keeping Danny Wilkinson's body out of sight. She stepped out of the car, smiling despite herself as she watched a couple of men struggle to drag a mattress from the back of a transit van. Beyond them, a woman was staring back at her from the open doorway of a house that looked to have seen better days. Certainly the weeds on the drive and the cracked front window spoke of neglect. The two men stumbled at the kerb, mattress wilting between them as they turned in opposite directions. There were a number of people hovering on pavements and in front gardens. Most of them had probably already seen the body but still wanted to see *more*.

Gwen, realising that she was staring at the woman in the doorway, gave an embarrassed smile and turned away. She ducked under the police tape and did her best not to appear hurt by how hostile the uniformed officers were on her arrival. The ranking officer on site simply waved at the small team of officers loitering around the body and walked out of the tent. Not a word was spoken as she was left on her own.

While the existence of Torchwood was still deemed 'secret', most of the police force knew of them, albeit only as 'that weird Special Ops lot'. Things had been too public of late, what with zombies marching the streets and people dropping like flies during the Welsh Amateur Operatic Contest. There was only a certain number of times the regular force could be kicked off an unusual crime scene by a handful of plainclothes operatives before two and two would be put together and a degree of resentment fostered. Nobody liked to be deemed unskilled for an investigation – whether they might want to pursue it or not – and there was no more effective phrase in the policing handbook for pissing off an officer than 'need to know only'.

Gwen squatted down next to Danny's body. The only overt physical damage was the shattered teeth and bloody gums where the boy's face had hit the ground, but that somehow made it worse. The surreal presentation and the palpable look of fear in his eyes was far more disturbing than anything so obvious as an open wound. How long had he been trapped like that? How long had he struggled? It made her itch just to think about it.

'Weird, huh?'

Jack's voice startled her and she wondered how long she'd been staring. 'You were quick.'

'Knew the way.'

He hissed air between his teeth as he took in the details of the body. 'That's just… *wrong*.'

It looked like he'd be using Alexander's pager sooner than he'd hoped.

Ianto parked the unmarked white van as close to the police tent as possible, grabbed a toolbox off the passenger seat and a white cotton face-mask from the glovebox. He hopped out of the van, only too aware that every net curtain within spitting distance was twitching as the locals ignored their usual afternoon telly for a slice of voyeurism closer to home. It must be like having Jeremy Kyle on all day. 'My boy in pavement scandal – lie detector special.' God, but he hated the suburbs…

He ducked down and entered the police tent.

'Hello, campers,' he said, putting down his toolbox. He cracked it open and pulled out a medium-sized chrome flask. 'Who's for coffee, then?'

'You read my mind,' Jack smiled and gave Ianto a wink.

'If the first thing that pops into your head when you see me is "hope that sexy devil put the kettle on before he left", then I can honestly say I don't know you half as well as I thought.'

'OK, it was the second thing that popped into my head.'

Ianto walked around Danny's body, sipping at his own drink. 'Poor sod,' he muttered before turning to Jack. 'When I got Gwen's message, I was already heading over here.'

'How come?'

'We picked up a huge chronon surge in the area. I cross-checked it with police reports and picked up news of Danny Wilkinson here.'

'The Rift?'

Ianto shook his head. 'Don't think so, the decay signature was different.'

Gwen began to make a sarcastic 'chat' gesture with her hands. 'Chronons… blah, blah… decay signatures… Try to remember we didn't all grow up playing with chemistry sets. Some of us had a life.'

Ianto smiled. 'Actually, I loved Action Men when I was growing up.'

'*Plus ça change*,' Jack said with a wink. 'Chronon particles are the fallout from temporal disruption,' he told Gwen. 'Like radiation. You can look at the way the particles degenerate to trace where they came from in the first place. The Rift has a very specific particle-decay signature. This didn't match it.'

'Thank you for the geekless subtitles.' She smiled. 'But how does weird time poo do that to a pavement?'

'Normally, I'd say it doesn't,' Jack replied. 'But I guess that's what we have to find out, isn't it?'

Ianto walked over to his toolbox and pulled out a small pen-shaped object.

'You might want to step back,' he warned Jack and Gwen. 'This thing's lethal.'

He placed his coffee at the far end of the tent before walking back over to the body. He twisted the object in his hand, and there was a high-pitched whine. He pointed it at the ground and began to trace a line around the body, a wedge of road surface – about four or five centimetres wide – vaporising as he passed. Finally, back where he started, he turned the machine off and placed it back in his toolbox.

'Pocket pneumatic drill?' asked Gwen. 'Handy.'

'I just bet it's sonic.' Jack smiled.

'Tosh's notes say "molecular", actually,' Ianto replied. 'It isolates the construction of the physical object you're pointing it at and removes that object completely within specified parameters. Bit like erasing stuff in Photoshop, only more dangerous… I sincerely doubt you can make your foot vanish at the ankle using Photoshop.'

Ianto walked out of the tent, went to the back of the van and unloaded a chunky-looking trolley, like a hospital gurney but more capable of off-roading. Wheeling it into the tent and alongside Danny's body, he squatted down and sighed.

'Unfortunately, nobody's thought of a cool way of doing the next bit.' He looked up at Jack. 'Cop your end, then,' he said. 'I'm not getting a hernia on my own.'

Jack came over and forced his fingers around the edge of pavement Ianto had left intact. The pair of them gave a roar as they hoisted it onto the trolley.

'Such manliness,' Gwen sighed. 'I'm almost overcome. Now hunt me bison.'

Neither of them graced her with a reply as they covered the body with a sheet and wheeled the trolley back out to the van.

Jack brushed fragments of grit from his palms as he watched Ianto pull away from the kerb and set off back to the Hub.

'I'll pay a visit to the kid's parents,' he said to Gwen.

'Sure?' she asked. It wasn't a part of the job any of them relished.

'Sure. Just set the boring paper trail running for me, would you? Traffic accident, no witnesses.'

'You sure we can contain this that simply? Loads of people are bound to have seen something.'

'Nobody'll believe it. The family are the only ones who'll cause a fuss. The neighbours will just make gossip, and nobody believes that.' He grinned. 'If I'm wrong we'll just add a little something to the water supply. Again. You want to ring PC Plod and tell them they can have their tent back or shall I?'

'I'll be politer,' she replied, pulling out her mobile.

'Yes you will.' He looked up at the sky where grim and weighty clouds clambered over one another, eager to give Cardiff a soaking. 'Tell 'em to make it quick if they want to be back indoors and curled up with their sweet tea and chocolate digestives before the rain comes.'

'Try and remember I used to be on the force, Jack,'

Gwen sighed, selecting Andy's phone number on her mobile speed dial.

'Yeah, but then you got a proper job. No more chasing scallywags and rescuing cats from trees for you.'

Gwen rolled her eyes, turning her back on him and getting into her car as Andy answered the phone.

Jack walked along the road, stopping in front of Jackson Leaves. It looked so tatty compared to the other houses in the street.

'Rotten tooth in an expensive smile,' he said. 'Scrub up, lick of paint – nobody would know how old you are.' He smiled at the idea. 'You and me both.'

He spotted movement at the front window, a momentary flash of red beyond the dirty, cracked glass. He turned away, not wanting to draw any more attention than they already had, and strolled back to the SUV.

Getting behind the wheel, he brought up the Wilkinson family's information on the built-in palmtop and was about to set the GPS when the street name clicked into place. He knew it; it was only just around the corner.

The first fat drops of rain exploded against the tinted glass of the windscreen, blurring the view outside to a dripping watercolour. He stared at the old houses as they appeared to melt. It was so easy to superimpose the city he once knew over the top of the one around him now. To look at these Edwardian stacks and remember them as new, as *modern*. But he fought against the temptation. He had always been a man – despite the affectation of his clothing – who tried to look forward. With the amount of history he held in his head, he could ill afford to do anything else. If he didn't box it up and lock it away, he would soon lose himself in it. Despite his best efforts, he still sometimes found himself panicking in a crowd, throwing second glances everywhere as the curve of a nose or twitch of a smile reminded him of someone he had once known. Ianto had once asked him how many lovers he had had. Jack had refused to answer, not to spare either of their feelings, more out of the fear that he might be unable to list them all. That would have hurt too much.

He put the wipers on their fastest setting, bringing the outside world back into sharp clarity, and drove to Danny Wilkinson's house.

Ianto pulled into the underground car park beneath the Millennium Centre, wincing as he always did when in the van. (He knew he had a spare few centimetres to clear the overhead barrier, but it didn't look like it, and he always expected the sound of tearing metal to accompany him into the gloom.) He hated having to sneak things into the Hub by this, the 'tradesmen's entrance'. He felt too exposed.

In the early days of Torchwood Cardiff, there had been access to the lower storage areas via submarine. *Submarine*… How cool was that? Who said things always improved over time?

He parked the van in its registered bay, stepped out

and checked around to make sure he was alone. He had made it his business to know all the users of the car park, their details filed away in his head. He used the Loci – or Memory Palace – technique, allocating visual triggers to the information so as to be able to store and recall everything quickly. He pictured the owners of each of the cars around him and then – using an expanded mental layout of the house he had grown up in – he checked each one of them off, placing them in a line of cupboards that he visualised in his old kitchen. For example, if he opened the cupboard just above the sink – the one with a Fiat 500 key-fob hanging from the handle – he would see David Thompson, the jolly young man who dealt with the intranet at the Welsh Assembly, sat on a tin of baked beans. In his hands he held the jack of clubs (Blackjack: giving his age as twenty-one in Ianto's system), and a photograph of Kelly Rowland (Thompson's flat-mate was called Kelly). If Ianto were to lean in and look at the time on Thompson's watch – a scratched souvenir from Disneyworld, Mickey waving his gloved hands cheerily as the seconds ticked away – he would see the hands pointing to five past nine: Thompson started work at nine and finished at five. It sounded complex, but Ianto found he could store huge quantities of information using the system, and storing information was a big part of what his life was about.

He finished his quick sweep around the bays on the lower level – everyone in their right place and nobody to see what he was up to – before opening the back doors of the van. The trolley's legs dropped down onto the concrete floor, taking the weight of Danny Wilkinson and the chunks of tarmac still attached to him. Ianto wheeled it over towards the door marked 'Private' that led to the Hub. He raised his face so the retinal-scanning software in the security camera could check him against access protocols. After a couple of seconds, the lock clicked to open and the doors parted slightly. Moving as quickly as possible – the doors were on a timer system of nine seconds – he wheeled the trolley into the short tunnel on the other side and pushed the doors firmly closed behind him.

The tunnel badly needed sorting out, the damp having encouraged moss to cluster around the light fittings like bushy green beards. It smelt bad too, though he was unsure whether there was much he'd be able to do about that. He hated getting behind in his housework. The Hub had gone to pot over recent months.

He walked through the weapons store – trying not to think about the amount of dusting *that* represented – then into the Hub itself.

Gwen had beaten him back.

'Took your time,' she said as he wheeled the trolley past her desk.

'I mind the speed limits when I have dead bodies in the back of the van,' he replied. 'Has Jack called that old friend of his yet?'

'Alexander Martin?' Gwen shook her head. 'Don't know. He was dealing with the boy's parents.'

'Oh.' Ianto nodded, lining the trolley alongside the upper railing of the Autopsy Room. 'The fun bit of the job.'

'Yeah.'

'Makes a change from you having to do it, I suppose.'

Ianto attached the slab of tarmac to a chain winch bolted into the ceiling, lifted it up and then lowered it into the Autopsy Room so that it was sat on the examination table. He ran down the stairs, lined the slab up and made sure the supports were tightened so the table could take the weight. He jogged back up the steps and over to his desk to check whether anything significant had occurred in his absence.

There had, and his face fell as he scanned his monitor screen. 'There's been another chronon surge…'

'Where?' Gwen asked, scooting over on her wheeled chair.

'Right on top of the last one.'

# FOUR

'That's horrible,' said the new woman.

'It is,' Gloria replied, sucking the pale blue smoke of her cigarette deep into her long-suffering chest. It wheezed under the assault, huddling behind the cotton of a knock-off designer blouse her husband had brought back from a 'business trip' to Thailand. As long as that was all he brought back, Gloria had long decided not to ask questions. 'And you can bet there'll be drugs behind it. They're *all* on drugs these days.'

Gloria peered through the privet hedge, trying to get a look at the woman who'd moved into Jackson Leaves. She looked young – though Gloria thought that about most people these days.

'I knew Joan,' she said. 'The lady that used to own the house.'

'My aunt.'

'Really?' Gloria relished the surprise she conveyed in her voice. 'She never mentioned you.'

There was little polite one could say to that of course.

'We weren't all that close.'

'So sad.' Gloria's casual spite had some bite left to it. 'It's terrible a woman of that age being so alone. Especially at the end.'

There was a slight pause from the other side of the hedge, and Gloria wondered if the young woman was going to argue. She hoped so; there was nothing she liked more than a good argument.

'At least she had her friends,' the young woman said. 'And neighbours of course. If you'll excuse me, I really must get on with the unpacking.'

Gloria let the woman go, too angry at having been outdone to think of a suitable reply. She ground her cigarette into the blue-granite gravel of her driveway, which was a considerable improvement on the cheap, weed-strewn grit of Jackson Leaves she assured herself, and turned her Ferragamo shoes – or at least a market-stall approximation of them – back toward the house. She couldn't loiter in the garden all day, after all.

Inside, she glanced at the clock in the kitchen and sighed. It was only four o'clock, and that limited her choices as far as slaking her thirst was concerned. Sometimes she just couldn't understand how time went past so slowly. It felt nearly time for bed, it really did.

She flipped the switch on the kettle and shuffled

through the box of exotic teas she kept mainly for show. She was sure there was an Earl Grey left in there, which was as much of a concession towards the exotic as she was willing to make if not in company. No, no Earl Grey… There was a 'Lady Grey' though… How different could it be? A little more long-suffering and capable of multitasking than the Earl, she imagined, pulling the cardboard tab from the top of the bag and dangling it from its clean white thread.

The kettle bubbled like her anger at the woman next door. It didn't have her patience, though, and was quick to boil. She poured the water on the teabag, cursing as a droplet of boiling water splashed from the cup and scalded the back of her hand. She slammed the kettle onto the worktop and seethed. She simply wasn't a woman used to not getting her own way in *everything*. Her entire life was constructed around her need to win. Certainly she had chosen her husband Trevor for his submissiveness; that and the fact he was able to earn the amount of money she deemed a bare minimum for comfortable living. If he didn't get a promotion soon, though, she'd have words. Penylan wasn't what it once was, and it was time they moved somewhere a little more exclusive. She didn't want to share a *postcode* with people like Danny Wilkinson, let alone have them turn up dead on her doorstep. Dear lord, she might as well be living in Splott.

Did you have milk with Lady Grey? She checked the little envelope it came in, but it didn't say. She supposed it didn't matter as long as she wasn't in company. A dash of skimmed milk and she was walking through to the lounge. She was so tired…

She put her tea on a side table, dropped down into her reclining, tan leather armchair and promptly burst into flames.

The fire burned with sufficient intensity to fix her to the spot, her muscles constricting in the heat and drawing her legs and arms to the chair as if she were gripping it in terror. In fact, there was too much pain for fear to even enter her head. She smelled herself cooking for a few moments before the heat seared the sensory cells in her nose. She saw a bubble of fat from her thigh pop and fizz – hadn't she always said she needed liposuction? – but then her eyes turned from weak brown to creamy white to nothing but rivers of hissing milk that cried themselves dry along her bursting cheeks. This was a blessing, there was nothing to be gained from watching her own flesh blacken and crack even as – bizarrely – the rest of the room escaped unscathed.

# FIVE

The windows appeared to be crying as much as Valerie Wilkinson, the rain trickling its way down the panes, dripping off the sill onto wilting blooms hammered down by the seasonal downpour.

'I'm sorry,' said Jack, unable to think of what else to say.

'No you're not,' she replied after a moment or two, dabbing at her running nose with a torn fist of kitchen roll. 'You didn't even know him. He's just a problem to solve.'

Jack stared at the floor, tracking the patterns in the lino as if following a maze that would let him escape from the unpleasant atmosphere.

'Yes,' he said eventually. 'But I will do my best to solve it, for what that's worth.'

She looked him up and down. 'I'm not sure it's worth much… I can't even remember who you said you were. You're not police.'

'No.'

'Why can't I remember?' she stumbled slightly, holding on to the work surface for support. 'I don't even remember letting you in…'

Jack got to his feet picking up the empty mugs from the table. 'You won't.'

Her legs gave way beneath her, so he put the mugs down quickly, moved to her side and supported her weight.

'It's OK,' he said. 'It just causes memory retardation, no other side effects.' *That we know of anyway*, he thought. He made her comfortable and lifted her chin slightly so he could look into her eyes. 'Your son died in a road accident. It was sudden and he felt no pain. There was nothing strange about the circumstances and, as sad as you are, there is no choice but to accept it and move on with your life.'

He sighed, pulled a handkerchief from his pocket – such an old-fashioned future-boy… who even carried handkerchiefs these days? – and began to rub down any of the surfaces he might have touched.

'You'll think your heart is broken,' he said, rubbing the armrests of the chair he had sat in and the surface of the pine table. 'That the death of someone who was once part of you can never be weathered, that you will just sit and rot…' He bit his lower lip. Who was it he was trying

54

to convince here, her or himself? 'But life goes on.' He stared right at her. 'You can, you *will*, know happiness again.'

His mobile began ringing, and there was a flicker in her eyes as it broke through the haze of the drug.

'Who are you?' she whispered, half-noticing him.

'I'm the last person you should ask that question,' he replied, pulling her eyelids gently closed with his fingers and answering the mobile. 'Hold on,' he said into the phone. 'You never saw me,' he whispered in Mrs Wilkinson's ear as she sank into sleep, moving quickly out of the house, wiping the door handles as he went.

Outside, he put the phone back to his ear. 'Hey, Gwen, sorry… Just readjusting the facts in the case of Danny Wilkinson.'

'No problem. Police reports altered and the usual news blankets in place at my end. Traffic accident, as you said.'

'Great. Thanks.'

'You may have another one on your hands, though. Huge chronon surge not a stone's throw from where we found the body, I've sent the coordinates to your PDA.'

'Great…' Jack was already climbing into the driver's seat and accessing the GPS software. 'Got it,' he said as the bookmark popped up onscreen. He dropped his mobile into his pocket and drove back towards Jackson Leaves. By now the rain was really thundering down, bouncing off the road surface and chasing leaves and litter along the gutter. He had to lean forward in his seat to see through the windscreen, even with the wipers on full speed. The police tent had been retrieved in his absence, and the excavated trench was overflowing with rainwater. God always cleans up his crime scenes.

He parked up and checked his PDA again. The surge appeared to be coming from the house almost directly opposite where Danny Wilkinson's body had been found. It hid its Edwardian heritage under layers of middle-class chic; faux-Japanese stone garden in front, Laura Ashley curtains visible through the lead-lined double-glazing. Come Christmas, Jack was in no doubt that ghastly fibre-optic threads would dangle from the guttering. Maybe a hollow-plastic Santa hiding within the shadows of the conifers, a brittle dwarf devoid of happiness or soul.

Jack pulled up the collar of his coat and clambered out of the SUV, dashing through the rain to the cover of the house's front porch. He rang the doorbell. No answer. Dropping to his haunches, he poked the letterbox open and peered through. There was little to see but a cream hallway leading through to the kitchen, where the owner was at work if the smell was anything to go by, Jack's mouth watered at the thick scent of roast meat. Pork, if he was any judge.

He rang the bell again and moved towards the lounge window, peering through the rain-splashed glass at the dark shape he could see sat in the far corner. Oh… Not pork.

He moved back to the front door but didn't bother with the bell, trying the handle just in case. The door was unlocked, so he pushed it open.

The smell of cooked meat washed over him. Now that he knew what it actually was, it made his belly groan. He pulled out his handkerchief, held it in the rain for a moment and then wrapped it around the lower part of his face so he looked like a Wild West outlaw. It didn't completely remove the smell, but it lessened it enough to walk inside without fear of throwing up. He took a few deep breaths of cool, wet air before moving into the lounge.

The body was black and pink, streaked with slicks of pearlescent body fat that caught what little light there was from the late-afternoon sun outside the window. Jack hunted through the inside pockets of his coat and pulled out a pair of latex gloves. With gritted teeth, he took hold of the woman's body and tilted it slightly in the chair. The scorch marks on the leather made it impossible to believe that the fire had started anywhere but the victim herself. Somehow she had burned while the rest of the room had remained untouched. Her skin crumbled and flaked under his fingers as he let her rock back to where she had been sitting. Looking around, he could see no other sign of damage; the ceiling bore a black mark where the smoke from her burning candle of a body had stained the paint, but that was all.

Suddenly the corpse flared again, knocking him on his back as he threw himself away from the blaze. The flames roared around the woman's body, small embers glowing inside her like the pulsing light of a firefly.

Then, as instantly as it had reignited, it vanished,

the flames disappearing to leave just the smouldering cadaver.

Jack's mobile rang again. He snatched it out of his pocket and answered. 'Let me guess,' he said straight away. 'Another surge?'

'Yes,' said Ianto. 'Same location as before but very brief. How did you know?'

'I was looking at it.' He got to his feet, keeping his distance from the body. 'I have a cremated corpse sat in front of me. Nothing's damaged but the chair it was sitting in.'

'Freaky.'

'Oh yeah… I'll bring the body in, but I want you to paper over the cracks for me.'

'No problem, bringing up the details now… The house belongs to Trevor Banks, he was a banker…'

'Deceased is a woman.'

'Most likely his wife then, Gloria. We'll confirm that when we have the body. I'll see if I can trace Mr Banks before he gets in your way.'

Through the window, Jack watched a BMW pull into the drive.

'Too late, he's here. Back soon.' Jack cut off the call and reached into his pocket for the Retcon. What an afternoon this was turning out to be…

# SIX

'It's warm,' Rob said, tugging off his paint-stained hoodie and tossing it into a corner of the room.

Julia wasn't listening. She was staring out of the bedroom window, watching the man she'd talked to earlier – the American in the big black car – run down next door's drive.

'What's he want now?' she wondered aloud. She hadn't expected an answer but Rob gave her one anyway.

'Who?' he asked, moving over to the window. Jack had vanished from sight.

'Nobody,' Julia answered, slightly embarrassed for speaking her thoughts aloud. 'Just some bloke that's been hanging around.'

'Hanging around?' Rob peered through the window, but there was nothing to see. 'He'll be hung from a lamp post if the Neighbourhood Watch catch him.' Turning to his wife he noticed her flinch slightly. 'What's up?'

She shook her head. 'Nothing.'

He wasn't so easily dissuaded. 'Yes there is. You've been funny all day. What is it?'

'Honestly, it's nothing. I didn't sleep well, that's all.'

Rob scratched at his stubble. She watched his dirty nails brush at the iron filings of his beard, wondering how many times she had seen him do it. It was an unconscious habit, like sticking the tip of his tongue out when he was concentrating or drumming his fingers on the arm of the sofa while they watched telly. She loved him, she really did, but she wished he'd shut up.

'Is it this place?' he asked.

'Who likes moving?' she replied, only too aware that she hadn't answered the question.

'Certainly not me,' said Steve from the doorway, 'and it's not even my bloody house.' He gave Rob a pointed look. 'Wardrobe ain't going to carry itself, is it?'

'Sorry, mate, right with you.' Rob gave Julia a pleading look, making sure she knew he wasn't satisfied with her lack of answer, and followed his friend downstairs.

Julia listened to their feet stomp along the creaking stairs, heard Steve make some dismissive comment and Rob bluster defensively. She would never understand what Rob saw in Steve. They had known each other since school and sometimes gave the impression they were still there, the bully and his flunky. It angered her. Rob wasn't weak, but Steve tried to make him so. He was that type of person, a man who grew tall by knocking down others. A hateful man.

The anger felt good, solid and constructive, directed at a physical object. Rather than an indefinable mood, it was a relief to feel something so honest. Rather than swallow it – and scold herself for being so hostile – she relished it.

She left the room as she heard them begin to climb back up the stairs with the flat-pack wardrobe. She had the sudden feeling that they would be able to tell what she had been thinking if they saw her. Her belly churned as her aggression became panic. She struggled to control her breathing. The sound of them walking upstairs was terrifying as she convinced herself that she would be in awful danger if they saw her.

She ran quietly into the spare bedroom, pulled open the chipped-formica doors of the built-in wardrobe and climbed inside. She sat down in the corner, breathing in the old, stale scent of a dead woman's clothes, mothballs and dust, and listening to the sound of her frantic heart pumping in her ears.

What was wrong with her? She felt as if every emotion she had was out of control. Scared, angry, confused… Was she having some kind of breakdown? The last time she'd felt like this was… well, there was no need to go there, that was months ago… and Rob had promised it would never happen again, that it had been a one-off mistake… Yes, thinking about *that* was only going to make things worse…

She tried to hear what Rob and Steve were doing. She could hear their voices but not their words. Were they talking about her? No, of course not. Why would they?

She could hear a dripping noise, a leaking tap making steel-drum percussion against the surface of an old bathtub. It sounded like it was coming from just outside the wardrobe. It must have been a trick of the acoustics, the noise bouncing off the old walls.

She became aware of the partly open door and felt another almost uncontrollable surge of panic, as if the slim crack of light alone were worthy of a scream. She forced herself to reach out and pull it closed – *carefully* – if her fingers poked out too far, who knew what might spot them and snap them off out of spite? When the door swung closed and she was wrapped in complete darkness, she brought her knees up to her chest and began inhaling slowly and deeply, trying to get her panic under control but not alert anything to her location by the noise of her breathing. She exhaled, and this was the hard part, opening her mouth wide and letting the air out as quietly as she could. She did this several times, picturing her pounding heart in the darkness and willing it to slow down. The sickness in her belly began to simmer and her jaw loosen. She pressed her back against the wall and imagined being able to turn to liquid, to just run into the cracks and the gaps between the floorboards, to escape… to be *nothing*.

The sound of dripping water persisted.

# SEVEN

'So, how *did* you get out?' Jack asked, pushing Alexander across Roald Dahl Plass. He caught a whiff of the burned woman from the lapels of his coat and was tempted to step out of the cover of the large umbrella and let the rain soak it off him. The SUV had needed fumigating by the time he'd got back to the Hub, the smell of Gloria Banks clinging to the upholstery like a takeaway. Today was not working out so well, and he wasn't sure that spending time with Alexander was likely to improve matters.

'I've been working on a homemade batch of perception-adjustment drugs for the last few weeks,' the old man replied, looking up at Jack with something approaching embarrassment. 'The nights are long and boring. After a while, you'll do anything to fill them.'

Jack steered the wheelchair towards the water tower.

'Should I be worried?'

'It's nothing major, just a basic distortion agent.' Alexander shifted in his seat. 'I dosed Pip Jarret's cocoa. He's currently waging war against the TV room furniture in the mistaken belief that it's a giant species of ant hell-bent on colonising South Wales. He provided quite the distraction.'

Jack centred the chair on the paving slab that marked the entrance to the Hub. 'Where did you get the chemicals to knock something like that up?'

'I brought some supplies with me.' Alexander held his hand up before Jack could interrupt. 'Nothing you need worry about. Besides, you can find most things naturally if you know what you're doing.'

'If I hear of colostomy bag explosives being sold on the open market, I'll know whose door to knock on.'

Jack tapped a button on his wrist-strap, and there was a jolt from beneath them. 'Wheelchair access,' he smiled as they vanished from Roald Dahl Plass and descended into the Hub.

Alexander was determined not to appear impressed as he tried to get his head around the layout of the place. He noted the presence of a hydroponics room and a large office, and several other rooms that he couldn't place at that distance. There was an ear-splitting screech from his left.

'Oh,' he sighed. 'You have a pterodactyl. How quaint.'

Jack laughed and the lift came to a jerky halt at the base of the tower. He shifted the wheelchair onto the metal gantry and pushed Alexander towards the Autopsy Room.

Ianto got up from his desk and headed towards them. 'Pteranodon, actually,' he said, frowning. 'Ianto Jones. You must be Alexander.'

'Yes, I must, mustn't I?' Alexander shook Ianto's hand and rolled his eyes as he spotted the look that passed between the young man and Jack. 'Tell him if he's going to roger you, the least he could do is get you an office of your own.' He waved at Ianto's workstation. 'Look at him, sat there in the middle of the entrance hall.' He looked up at Jack. 'Bet *you've* got your own office.'

'Well…'

'Thought as much. Bet you don't use it for much more than looking at porn and listening to Glenn Miller, either.'

Jack gave Ianto a look that begged for help and wheeled Alexander towards the Autopsy Room. They came to a halt at the top of the curved flight of metal steps, and Alexander sighed, looking at the route down.

'Didn't think *that* through, did you?'

Gwen stepped through the main Hub gate with a stack of pizzas in her hands. She watched as Ianto and Jack carried the old, swearing man and his wheelchair into the Autopsy Room.

'Hello,' she said once they had reached the bottom of the steps. 'Would this be the temporary medical help, by any chance?'

'Very temporary!' Alexander shouted. 'I've resigned twice since these Neanderthals started manhandling me. A man of my qualifications gets used to being treated with a certain amount of respect!'

'Oh, shut up, you miserable old git,' Jack said with a chuckle. 'If I'd known I was employing Old Man Steptoe, I'd have thought twice.'

Ianto wheeled Alexander over to the examination table which Jack was lowering to a more practical working height.

'Thank you, young man.' Alexander gave Ianto a smile and a half-wave towards Gwen. 'Nice to meet you, probably.'

'Gwen Cooper,' she replied, 'and I'm afraid there's nothing nice about what you're going to see under there.' She pointed at the table.

'I've seen things you wouldn't believe, my dear,' Alexander replied. 'Walked knee-deep in the meat of alien battlefields. Worked the front line of a war fought by species advanced enough to liquidise an enemy at the flick of a switch.' He looked up at Gwen. 'Have you any idea how disconcerting it is when your patients arrive in the form of broth?' He tugged the sheet free, leaving it to fall to the ground, where Ianto was quick to tidy it away. 'Though I must admit,' Alexander continued, looking at Danny Wilkinson's body, 'this is certainly *bizarre*.'

He began to wheel himself around the table. 'All external signs of violence – the shattered mouth, the chafing where the skin has torn against the tarmac in his efforts to free himself – would seem to make it clear that death was due to either shock or suffocation.'

'Suffocation?' Ianto asked.

'You try breathing a pavement and see how far your lungs get.' He checked the boy's mouth. 'Given the angle of his neck and throat and the fact that he obviously took some time to die, I'm assuming the pavement somehow infiltrated his mouth but not the rest of him.' He looked at Jack. 'If the pavement had appeared inside the rest of his body, he would have died instantly. This leads us to the conclusion that it must have been the pavement that lost physical cohesion and not the boy.'

'Oh yeah,' muttered Ianto, placing the carefully folded sheet away in a drawer. 'It'll be that old liquid pavement problem again. The council *were* looking into it, I believe…'

Alexander chuckled and nodded his head towards Ianto. 'I *like* him. He definitely deserves his own office.'

'Is there a list?' Gwen said. 'Somewhere I can put my name down? I'd like a pot plant, too, if the budget will stretch.'

'Ooh…' Ianto smiled. 'There's a Venus Flytrap in the containment chamber you can have. Saves me having to feed it.'

Jack looked at Gwen. 'Careful, it eats thirty kilos of fresh meat a day. We found it in the Brecons after following up reports on missing hikers.'

'It just *loves* Kendall Mint Cake.' said Ianto.

'God save me from your world,' Alexander muttered,

running his fingers along the surface of the tarmac. 'I'm going to need access to your chemical stores and maybe that greenhouse upstairs.'

'Sure,' Jack replied. 'What are you after?'

'I want to mix something up that will dissolve all this tarmac and leave the body intact. You might want to take a sample first. Run some broad-range scans.'

Ianto held up a finger, walked to a drawer, pulled a lump hammer out and struck the edge of the tarmac with enough force to chip a piece off.

Gwen stared at the mallet. 'Don't you *ever* ask to tap my knee with that.'

Ianto smiled. 'Good for tenderising plant food.'

'And in box number two…' Jack said, yanking open one of the large drawers to reveal the body of Gloria Banks.

'Burn victim?' Alexander shrugged. 'What's the connection?'

'The location. They were found only metres and hours apart,' Jack replied. 'Also a large chronon surge at the time and location of death in both cases.'

'I'm a physician and chemist, not a physicist,' Alexander noted, 'so it's not really my field. However,' he smiled, 'I'm also excruciatingly clever and in love with the sound of my own voice, so I'll comment anyway. Chronon particles aren't proactive enough to do damage themselves, even in extraordinarily high doses. They are a symptom not a cause.'

'Agreed,' Jack replied, 'but they're also our only lead to

what's going on.'

Ianto dashed up the stairs and over to his desk, reappearing next to Gwen on the railings. He held up what appeared to be a mobile phone. 'This can be used to trace chronon particles.' He looked at all three of them in turn and shrugged as they didn't say anything. 'I'll get my coat then, shall I?'

Later, Ianto sat down in the dry of a bus stop, eating fish and chips in the company of a couple of empty crisp packets, a carrier bag, several crushed beer cans and a stray cat that eyed him – or rather his fish – from the other side of the shelter.

'There's no end to the glamour of life in Torchwood,' he told the cat. 'It's just like James Bond except more... really, really *crap*.'

Perhaps the cat didn't believe him. Certainly it was happy to risk the rain until he threw it a few flakes of cod. 'Thank you,' he said, as it decided to hang around. 'I hate eating alone. The menu isn't what it could be either.' He held up the fish. 'You should try Brenda's on St Mary Street. Much tastier.' He smiled. 'The service isn't bad either. Ask for Patrick.'

He'd spent the last couple of hours wandering up and down the streets, trying to pick up a trace of chronon particles. He'd hung around the road where Danny Wilkinson's body had been found but, noticing a few curtains beginning to twitch, had decided to head up to the high street and keep his head down for an hour.

Last thing he wanted was a slanging match with nosy suburbanites.

He flung the cat as much of his fish as he could dig free of the batter and ketchup mush he had created and dumped the rest in a wastepaper bin. Digging a wedge of serviettes from his jacket pocket, he began to scrub his hands clean with rainwater and dedication.

He decided it was probably safe to head back towards the Land of Twitching Curtains. He should give the place another thorough sweep for an hour and then call it quits. Opening his umbrella, he stepped back out into the rain.

A group of kids were sheltering under the awning of a convenience store. Cigarettes and a two-litre bottle of strong cider passed between their lips, the usual night-time sports whatever part of town you were in. A smart-looking woman gave them a wide berth as she aimed for the store entrance. A couple of wolf whistles followed her inside, but she ignored them.

'Look at that poof,' one of them said as Ianto walked past. He tried to think of something scathing to shout back, but he could come up with nothing that didn't sound desperate rather than witty, and he didn't want to give them more ammunition.

He crossed the road and tried to walk as nonchalantly as possible. Ridiculous… He'd faced off alien invasions with a quip and a spring in his step, but put him up against a bunch of chavs and his nerve went. Pathetic.

He heard them wolf whistle again and turned to see the smart-looking woman leaving the shop with a bottle of wine in her hand. She marched straight into the road, taking as wide an angle away from the kids as she could while still heading home. 'Fancy joining the party?' one of the boys shouted, much to the hilarity of the others. 'Swap you some of your booze for a bit of tongue!' He waggled it for her, but she kept her attention fixed firmly on the road.

Little bastards. Ianto was walking back towards them when the scanner in his pocket began squealing. The woman stared at him, a hint of panic in her eyes. Ianto clawed the scanner out, trying to look both reassuring and apologetic.

'The poof's got a rape alarm!' one of the kids shouted. 'He should be so lucky!'

The scanner was going haywire, and Ianto could make neither head nor tail of what it was trying to tell him. He looked up, hoping to at least reassure the panicking woman. He smiled at her and there was obviously enough sincerity there as she was beginning to smile back when something collided with her from behind. Her body spasmed into a star shape that would have been almost funny were it not for the look on her face and the distinct cracking of bone that carried between the electronic bleeps of the scanner. Her umbrella – a small affair decorated with autumn leaves – popped into the shape of a cocktail glass and fell from her hand. She appeared to hover for a few seconds, then she fell forwards and began to roll, over and over, coming straight at him.

The kids outside the shop were running away in the

opposite direction, they could see that the night had taken a bad turn and they'd be best placed anywhere but here.

As the woman drew close, tumbling over herself, arms and legs spinning at angles that proved them free of their sockets, Ianto became aware of another noise between the bleeping of his scanner: the grinding of metal wheels on tracks. There was a taste of ozone on the air, as faint as a memory of childhood fairs.

Just before the ghost of a tram hit him, Ianto had the good fortune to disappear, leaving behind the woman, who came slowly to a halt as the present day reasserted itself.

# EIGHT

And still the feeling wouldn't go away. Steve had left for the prior commitment of a pub quiz in town, and Rob was at the point where he was so tired all he could do was stand and stare at the mess around him without being able to usefully interact with it. Last time she'd seen him, he had been staring at a half-built wardrobe, clearly wishing the bloody thing would just have the decency to screw *itself* together.

Julia was drinking wine. Not enough to become as wrecked as the house, but enough to make her not care so much about the mess.

The mess and the ghost.

Not that she would let herself use that word.

She kept seeing him, the fat man. She had caught a glimpse of his colourful tie – red paisley, autumnal swirls – while filling the kitchen cupboards with their mismatched crockery. She had seen him in the bathroom mirror as she filled the cupboard with half-full bottles of medicine and ran her thumb across the ageing bristles of their toothbrushes. She had seen him in the shadows of the top-floor landing as she had dumped yet another box of belongings she couldn't face in one of the spare rooms. She had even felt his breath on the back of her neck as she had taken down the thick, musty curtains that hung in the main lounge. It had smelled of fried onions and sweat.

God, but she wished he would go away.

Rob rolled the screwdriver from one hand to the other and imagined punching the man who invented flat-pack furniture squarely on the nose. Throwing the screwdriver on the floor, he rubbed at his face and tried to find the energy to get on. He picked up the instructions – which were even more difficult to read now that he had crumpled them into a ball and thrown them across the room – flattened them out and stared at Fig 4b until his brain began to melt.

He could hear the sound of running water and felt an urge to ditch all this and go and help Julia have the bath she must be running. Better not, she'd only take the mick if he left the wardrobe unfinished.

*Take bolt X and make of insert into apartures F with use of key of provision.*

'Key of provision'? Don't be an idiot, did they think

he was stupid enough not to guess that the Allen key wouldn't be in the box as promised? He had a set of his own, thank you very much.

*Making care of not for bend, with end flash agin rear panel, take bolt MM and…*

'And stick it up our translator's arse?' Rob muttered, rubbing his eyes again. It would be easier without the damn things, surely?

The rush of the bath taps continued to call to him.

He threw the instructions to the floor and walked over to the wardrobe, placing his hand on one side. It swung into a skewed parallelogram, and he was quick to right it before the strain pulled one of the bolts out of the soft wood. 'Damn thing may as well be made from cardboard,' he muttered, turning the frame around so that he might be able to fix some strengthening slats to the back of it.

The sound of running water changed from the deep sloshing of a filling bathtub to the patter of water spilling onto wood and tile. It was overflowing.

'Bloody hell!' Rob growled, his patience finally snapping. The water was bound to soak through and damage the floor below. *More* work…

He kicked the wardrobe hard in his anger, almost relishing the sound of splitting chipboard as he stormed out of the bedroom. He drew to a halt on the landing as he realised the sound of water wasn't coming from the bathroom but rather the spare bedroom. He changed direction, opened the door and stared at the impossibility that flooded the room beyond it. He could see a bathtub, a big old metal affair, overflowing with the water that rushed into it from ghostly taps. He looked down at his feet and watched the impossible water touch the toes of his boots and then roll around them as it found its way past, flowing beyond him and towards the open door. He lifted his foot and the water actually dripped, thick like mercury, from the bottom of his boot. He rubbed the sole. It felt dry. Suddenly his entire body cramped and then, right in front of him, having walked *through* him, was a naked woman. She walked towards the bathtub, stepped inside, dropped to her knees and then opened her hand to reveal the glint of a razor blade.

'Don't…' Rob whispered, stepping forward even as the image of the woman lowered her arms into the warmth of the water and began to cut. He tried to grab at her but her flesh slipped through his fingers with the stinging sensation of stroking a nettle. Blood began to fill the tub and she turned and lay back in the water so that he was leaning over her like a lover. He dropped to his knees, tears coming to his eyes as he continued to try and grab the dying woman in front of him.

'Julia!' he shouted, though whether he wanted her to help or simply to prove that what he was seeing wasn't for his eyes alone, he couldn't say. 'Julia!'

She appeared at the doorway behind him, her hand shooting to her mouth to stifle a shout. That was all the proof he needed that she shared this hallucination. He became aware of the feeling of water on the palms of his hands, the soft brush of the woman's skin, as if she were

76

becoming more real… He looked down and watched as a damp shadow of water spread across the legs of his jeans and the belly of his shirt. He made another grab at the woman and the water exploded around him, splashing his face and blooding his tongue with the taste of copper, before it vanished leaving him soaking wet in a bone-dry room.

'You saw that?' he asked Julia once he could find the strength of mind to speak.

'Yes,' she replied, but could think of nothing else to say.

They stayed there in silence for a few minutes, Julia watching as Rob started to shiver in the cooling, impossible water that covered him from head to toe. Thinking of something she could do, she left the doorway and went to the airing cupboard for a towel. Opening the door, her shocked silence snapped and she screamed as a well-dressed young man fell out of the airing cupboard and onto the floor at her feet.

# NINE

Gwen parked the car and sat for a few minutes watching the rain paint patterns with the streetlights on the windscreen.

She often sat in the car for a while before going up to the flat she shared with Rhys. These few minutes of silence were an emotional airlock between her working life with Torchwood and her marriage. When she had first started, she had found it near impossible to keep the two apart in her head. After joining the police force, she had gone through a period of fear that was common in new recruits: the job gave you a heightened awareness of what bad things the world could offer and the result was that, for a while at least, you became convinced danger was around every corner. That feeling had trebled when joining Torchwood. She would watch Rhys sleeping and imagine him a mess of Weevil bites. It just felt so damn dangerous in Cardiff, and she couldn't quite believe that the violence wouldn't reach them. How could it not? It was everywhere…

She had calmed down eventually of course. She would have gone mad otherwise. When your day can be anything from the living dead to extraterrestrial infections, you need to be able to compartmentalise. This was part of that, just leaning back in the car seat, closing her eyes and pushing it all away. Today, the image that stuck to the back of her eyes, like chewing gum, was that of Danny Wilkinson's serrated teeth as they tried to chew their way through tarmac. She had seen worse things, but there was something about it that made her belly churn more than normal. It was a pain she could almost relate to… *Almost.* There was the smell of Gloria's body too, a black sweetness that clung at the back of her throat. She bit her lip, forcing the thought away before it made her gag.

She ferreted in the door compartments for a brolly but came up with nothing more useful than an empty water bottle and a crisp packet. Grabbing them for the bin, she opened the door and made a dash for dryness.

Upstairs, having been alerted by the sound of the car engine, Rhys watched Gwen out of the window, as he opened a bottle of chilled Sauvignon Blanc – her favourite, so why would he buy anything else? He'd noticed a long time ago how she sat outside for ages after returning from work. The first time he'd caught her at it, he'd been terrified, his head buzzing with all the imagined reasons she might be nervous about coming in. Convinced she was going to confess to an affair by the time she finally appeared, he'd been on edge all night, snappy with her, waiting for the axe to fall. Of course it never had. Wasn't he always his own worst enemy in the end?

He poured two glasses of wine as he heard her feet on the stairs and the involuntary moan as she shook cold rainwater from her hair. As the door opened, he put a glass in her hand and a kiss on her lips.

'Now that's service!' she laughed, still pulling her damp hair away from her face.

'Damn right. Now sit down, and I'll fetch a towel for your hair.'

She took off her boots and did as he asked, taking a sip of the chilled wine and nudging the James Bond boxed set that was on the carpet with her foot.

'Been getting pointers?' she asked as he came back with the towel.

'Eh?'

She nodded at the DVDs.

'Oh, aye… Passes the time while you're saving the world.' He smiled and draped the towel over her head. 'Have you?'

'Have I what?' she replied rubbing at her wet hair.

'Saved the world of course? It happens so often I sometimes forget to ask.' He grinned as he headed to the kitchen.

'No, not today,' she called after him, draping the towel across her lap. 'Today was not a good day.'

Rhys came back and looked at her. 'Tell me about it.'

She smiled to see how much he clearly loved her. 'You don't want to know.'

'I do, of course I do. Come on, Gwen, what sort of husband would I be if I wasn't here to offload on?'

'Two people died,' she said. 'One was only a young lad…the other a woman.'

'Do you know who did it?' Rhys asked.

'We don't even know whether it was natural or not,' Gwen admitted. 'For all we know, there could be more by the morning.'

'But you still came home.'

Gwen smiled. 'I missed you.'

Rhys nodded, returning to the kitchen and opening the oven. 'That and the fact you were starving and knew that I was cooking.' He removed the baking tray and dropped it onto the work surface. 'Spare ribs!'

Gwen caught the smell wafting from the oven and was on her feet and running towards the bathroom.

Rhys bit his lip as the sound of her throwing up worked its way back to the kitchen.

'Or maybe you're not that hungry after all,' he muttered, putting down his oven glove and stepping through to the bathroom.

'I'm sorry,' Gwen said, wiping her mouth and flushing the toilet. 'It was the smell… The woman I said about, she burned to death and… Sorry, I just can't.'

Rhys sat down on the edge of the bathtub and stroked her hair. 'Don't be silly, not your fault… I just wish… I… I don't know.'

'What?'

'Wish I knew all the right things to say to make you feel better,' he said. 'It's not like other people, is it? If your wife comes home from a bad day at the office you listen to her bitch about her boss, say all the right things and help her get it off her chest. With you… Well, what can I say? "Sorry you've had another day of death and violence, love, fancy a takeaway and a rented movie to take your mind off it?" There's just nothing I can do is there? How can I help you deal with the sort of thing that's your day? I just feel useless sometimes.'

Gwen hugged him. 'You're not useless at all, you're lovely. In fact you're *perfect*.'

He smiled. 'Oh aye, you're right actually. I forget how great I am sometimes.'

'You do,' she said, squeezing his hand.

They sat there for a moment, holding each other's hands.

'Go on,' Rhys said eventually.

'Go on what?'

'Go back to work,' Rhys replied. 'You'll feel better if you just work through it. I know you, come the early hours you'll stumble on something and it'll all start making more sense and *then* you can walk away a bit, knowing you've done something.'

Gwen stared at him and felt her love for the man deepen

even further than she could have thought possible. 'What did I ever do to deserve you?' she said.

'No idea,' he grinned. 'You're just the luckiest woman in all of Cardiff, I suppose.'

'In the whole world.'

'Whole universe!'

'Now you're talking.' He kissed her on the cheek. 'Go on, I mean it. I won't even miss you. I've got wine, extra dinner and more action films than I can shake a machine gun at. You'll only cramp my style. I had the perfect evening planned before you showed up and dripped all over the sofa.'

She kissed him again, hard, and nodded.

He sat there a little longer as he listened to her grab her car keys and head back out of the door.

'I lied,' he said to himself. 'I miss you more than you ever know.'

Getting up, he headed back into the kitchen to plate up his dinner.

Gwen stepped back into the Hub and walked over to her workstation.

She could hear the sound of Alexander still working away in the Autopsy Room, the occasional swear word or grunt wafting up the stairs. She wondered where Jack knew him from. He hadn't volunteered the information, of course. Did he ever? The old man had just been presented to them as 'someone he knew', and that would have to be enough. Not that she didn't trust Jack, but – and maybe it was the old copper in her – she liked to know who she was dealing with, didn't like secrets. Never mind, secrets were Jack's preferred currency and she supposed one day she would get used to it.

She booted up her computer and settled herself in her chair. While she might not be able to find out anything about Alexander just now, there were certainly more pressing mysteries to hand and hopefully they *were* something she could figure out. After all, with the facilities she had at Torchwood there was very little she couldn't discover given a little time and enough processing power to run a small country. She had never got over how wonderful Torchwood's search database was. Having worked in law enforcement, she knew that – whatever films said to the contrary – cross-referencing evidence was not the same as Googling. You didn't just put in two or three search strings then get presented with a handful of potential suspects. It took hours and – worse than that – there was no guarantee that you'd find *anything* useful at the end of it. Actually, scratch that, it was *exactly* like Google… But not with Torchwood. The database was composed of every conceivable registry: civil, law enforcement, even intelligence services – her computer access alone was enough to have her assassinated as a security risk in nineteen countries.

She tapped in the address and then sat back, wondering what might help to narrow it down. It was depressing to admit there was nothing… The state of the body perhaps? No, that might make things too specific. Chronons?

Perhaps. She tapped them in and then deleted it again. Just check the address, start wide and narrow down.

She rummaged in her workstation for the little jar of instant coffee she kept hidden from Ianto, but it was empty. She went to persuade the coffee machine to give her a cup while the computer gave itself a good talking to. She tapped her nails impatiently on the side of the machine as it bubbled and gurgled its way towards a gritty cappuccino. She was sure Ianto had sabotaged the thing to ensure it never came close to competing with his own finely crafted caffeine doses. Perhaps he injected it with river silt. Finally, it dribbled apologetically into a mug, which Gwen carried back to her desk.

Her monitor was attempting not to look smug as it offered an alphabetical list of news reports and police files relating to the road in Penylan. She was surprised by how many there were, even more so once she realised they all related to the same building: the house she had seen the young couple moving in to. But that was nothing compared to the final revelation her computer had to offer. She stabbed at the button of her desk intercom, scanning the text on her screen as she waited for Jack to answer.

'Hey, Gwen,' barked the intercom speaker. 'Please tell me it's not morning already.'

'We need to talk,' Gwen replied. 'Boardroom, twenty minutes.'

'OK,' Jack said as he strolled into the Boardroom. 'Brighten up my night and tell me you've found something we can go beat up. Dealing with Alexander's given me lots of aggression to work off.'

'Sit down,' Gwen replied, connecting her PDA to the projector, 'and shut up.'

'I just *love* bossy women,' Jack replied, though his smile soon faded as her mood reached him.

The projection screen began to fill with images: an elderly lady with skin as pale as a bed-sheet; a skinny girl, little to her but cheekbones and sadness; a long-haired surfer-type, beard grown thick to hide his youth; a glamorous woman, headscarf and big sunglasses; a myopic balding man, like a mole in a pullover... The faces kept coming, fourteen in all, until one final portrait made Jack sit forward.

It was his own.

'What have all these people got in common?' asked Gwen.

Jack could only shrug, though a suspicion rolled around in his head that was confirmed when she cued up the next image.

'They all lived here,' she said, pointing to the photo of the Edwardian house. 'Jackson Leaves, built in 1906 and trouble ever since, it seems. Were you going to mention it?'

'That I lived there?' Jack replied. 'Probably not... It hardly seemed relevant. I've been around, you know... There's not many parts of Cardiff I don't know intimately.'

'Not many of its residents either,' Gwen muttered.

'My point is, just because I used to live nearby doesn't mean Danny Wilkinson's death was anything to do with me.'

'Maybe not, but I'd be willing to bet that something about that house is connected.' Gwen tapped the trackpad on her PDA, and the line of faces reappeared on the projection screen. 'It has a history, Jack,' she pointed at the faces. 'You're the odd one out here. Know why?'

Jack shrugged.

Gwen stared at him for a moment, as if trying to decide whether she believed him or not. 'You're the only one who's still alive,' she said. 'The rest of them died in the house.'

'*All* of them?' said Jack. 'That's long odds.'

'*Ridiculously* long, and they don't include people like Danny who died on the doorstep.' Gwen stared at the faces on the screen. 'The odds get worse,' she continued, pointing at the old lady. 'Joan Bosher. Lived there over thirty years before a heart attack sent her packing, she's the one who left it to the young couple we saw moving in yesterday. She's the only person on this list whose death could have been natural. The rest… no way.'

She pointed at the thin woman. 'When Joan Bosher originally moved in, she let out rooms to lodgers. This is one of them: Kerry Robinson, librarian and aspiring poet, opened her wrists in the bathtub.'

She moved her finger to the long-haired man. 'Richard Hopkins, trainee hairdresser in Barry, also a lodger. He went berserk with a croquet mallet at a local pub.' Gwen glanced at her PDA to remind her of the name. 'The Hop and Kilderkin... Ran back to the house and put a pair of hairdressing scissors through his left eye.' She pointed at the woman in a headscarf. 'Michelle Sillence, interior designer – owned the place before Joan with an intention to renovate. She didn't so much as open a pot of paint...'

Gwen sighed and rubbed at her tired face. 'She was found hanging from one of the roof joists in the attic, pigeons had made a meal of her face. We've got the lot, drowned, shot, stabbed...' She gestured vaguely at the faces in front of them. 'All of them died... *badly* at Jackson Leaves.'

Jack stared at the screen. 'It was a nice house...'

'You – and possibly Joan Bosher – are the only ones who think so. As much as it makes me cringe to say it, something about that house attracts violence and death.'

'So what is it, and why were Joan and I not affected?'

'You telling me that you live a violence-free life?'

Jack stared at her for a moment. 'I suppose not.'

'For all we know, you just might not have noticed.'

Jack's mobile rang. He pulled it from his pocket and flipped it open. 'Yeah?'

Gwen watched the smile falter on his face. 'In your what?' he asked before his expression changed from confusion to concern. 'I know where it is,' he snapped. 'I'll be right over.'

He closed the phone.

'Ianto's been found unconscious,' he said. 'You'll never guess *where*…'

# TEN

It was almost as if the ghostly water had frozen Rob, stuck on his knees staring at the spare bed that had reasserted itself in the room. It seemed solid enough. The creases of the off-white sheet, the loose silken threads on the embroidered base, a plastic badge with the brand-name on it turned yellow over the years. It seemed ridiculous to think that an old bathtub had occupied the same space only a few minutes ago.

He looked down at his wet shirt, a hint of pink in the damp of the white fabric. That was real enough. He heard Julia leave the room, but his mouth felt soft and useless, and he couldn't believe it would ever be used for speaking again. This proved untrue, as the minute he heard her scream he was shouting her name and getting to his feet.

She was standing in the hallway, staring down at a man in a three-piece suit who lay unconscious at her feet.

'He's real,' she said, nudging him with her foot.

Rob dropped to his haunches and rolled the man onto his back. There was a white sheen to his hair and eyebrows, small crystals on his cheeks and forehead. Rob touched the skin gently. 'Ice,' he whispered. 'He's covered in bloody *ice*.'

Julia made a slight groaning noise and leaned against the airing cupboard door. 'What's going on?' she said, not expecting an answer.

Rob didn't feel up to giving her one. 'He's alive,' he said, feeling the man's pulse. He frisked through the man's pockets, pulling a wallet out of his jacket. The wallet was sparse and ordered, unlike his own graveyard of receipts and store benefit cards; there was a crisp twenty-pound note, a plain black credit card and a business card featuring a simple message: 'The bearer of this card is Ianto Jones. If found, please dial 000 and wait for a response.'

'That's not even a proper number,' Julia said, reading over Rob's shoulder.

'One way to find out,' he replied, pulling his mobile out of his pocket and dialling three zeroes. Someone answered almost straight away, and Rob raised his eyebrows at Julia. 'Hello, erm… My name's Rob Wallace, and I've just found someone called Ianto Jones in my airing cupboard.'

The other person obviously commented on this. Julia watched a flash of embarrassment cross her husband's face before anger reasserted itself. 'I know it sounds bloody mad,' he replied, 'but it seems to be the night for that around here. There was a… ghost…'

It was the first time the word had actually occurred to Rob, and the minute it fell out of his mouth, he wished he could swallow it again – it sounded stupid and embarrassing, the sort of thing a child would say. 'Look, it doesn't matter. He's alive but he's out of it. Freezing cold and… well, I don't know… he seems OK, but he shouldn't be here, that's for sure. I'm in Penylan, a house called Jackson Leaves…' Rob looked startled, holding the phone away from his head.

'He hung up on me,' he said. 'Says he knows where we are, and he's coming over.'

'Is that a good thing?' Julia asked.

Rob didn't know, shaking his head and trying to think of what to do next.

'We should try and warm him up,' said Julia. 'Maybe…' She'd been about to suggest a bath but had then been unable to face the idea. 'I don't know, get a fire going or something… Wrap him in blankets.'

Rob thought for a moment, unable to decide whether he was happy helping this stranger or not. He gave an irritated growl as he realised he couldn't *not*. 'All right then, let's get him downstairs. You grab his legs…'

Julia did. 'God,' she exclaimed before letting him go again. 'He's *freezing*.'

'I know.'

Rob was gritting his teeth, hooking his arms under

93

Ianto's armpits and trying to lift the man's dead weight. 'Heavy, too.'

Julia took the hint and grabbed Ianto's legs again, ignoring the cold feel of him on her palms.

She went backwards, shuffling awkwardly, feet splayed out for balance as Rob grunted his way after her.

'Going to put my back out,' Rob muttered, trying to get a better hold of Ianto. He didn't notice the shadow that fell across them from the top of the stairs, but Julia did. She knew who she would see when she looked up, could tell by how *wide* the shadow was.

'Weird,' Rob said. 'I can smell onions…'

'Just keep going,' Julia replied, refusing to look at the fat man above them as he licked his lips and wiped the sweat from his palms on the shiny breast of his pinstripe suit.

They got to the foot of the stairs, and Rob turned around, stretching his back and dragging Ianto into the lounge.

He laid Ianto on the sofa and then came dashing towards her.

'I think I saw some fire stuff in the cupboard under the stairs,' he said, rubbing his hands together from the cold. He saw a look on her face that worried him. 'Don't,' he said, shaking slightly. 'If I stop, I'll lose it. Seriously, I've got to keep moving, don't think… just *do*.'

He pushed past her and jogged to the cupboard, yanking the door open and rifling through the junk inside. They were going to have to throw most of this crap away, whatever Julia might say. There were boxes of newspapers and magazines, a stack of yellowing paperbacks, an old croquet set (though one of the mallets had clearly been damaged at some point, as the shaft was wrapped in plastic tape), an old Dansette record player… so much rubbish. He grabbed a box of the newspapers and spotted a couple of carrier bags of dried kindling. No coal or larger logs, though; no doubt they were outside. They could stay there. He'd build the thing out of sticks and newspaper, rather than go hunting for them; there was plenty of it, after all. He took it all through to the grate, closing the lounge door behind him, and began snapping fire-lighters over scrunched-up balls of decade-old newspaper.

'What are we doing?' Julia asked.

Rob shook his head. 'That man will be here soon.'

'So?' Julia responded. 'For all we know he's… I don't know.' She hugged herself. 'He might be no help at all. I mean… *Jesus*… What's happening, Rob?'

Her voice was getting more high-pitched, she was losing the numbness that had kept her going, and now she just wanted to start lashing out.

Rob was sinking into himself, his fingers slowly ferreting around in a matchbox for a fresh match to light.

'Why are we even still here?' she asked.

Rob couldn't give her an answer, slowly striking a match against the crumbling sandpaper. The match snapped, unlit. He hunted for another.

'*Seriously*,' Julia continued, 'this is ridiculous. Please tell me you have the van keys? We could be driving up the road and away from here…'

The second match flared.

Julia walked towards the lounge door, determined to get out of the building.

The door began to vibrate in its frame, wood hammering against wood, hard enough to bring dust from the ceiling. Julia gave a surprised yelp and Rob dropped the match to the floor, running to her side and grabbing her protectively. They squeezed each other as the banging continued, a pounding that seemed to move from the door across the walls and ceiling, like a colossal hammer being brought down on the house all around them.

The television switched on, its screen filled with static, the white noise of the speaker drowning out the faint crackle of a building flame where the dropped match was setting fire to the rug. *Anything* can be heard in the chaos of white noise, whispers and the delicate shapes of words beneath the crackle and pop. If Rob and Julia had been feeling rational, they would never have believed they heard voices in the speaker.

They were not feeling rational.

Rob's fingers dug into the pale flesh of Julia's shoulder, pressing bright white crescents into the pink of her skin as the house continued to beat around them. Julia wasn't in the least surprised to catch the smell of onions on her tongue, she had no doubt the fat man was pressing his weight against the other side of the door at that very moment.

It was Ianto, opening eyes crusty and chill with the rime of frost, that spotted the danger coming from the lit rug. He rolled off the sofa, an awkward grunt knocked out of him as his limbs refused to hold him up, dragged himself by his elbows and rolled onto the tiny fire, his damp suit hissing as it extinguished the flames. His mind was slow to function, but somewhere right on the periphery of his awareness – and even above the noise of the television – he heard a familiar engine outside the house, the heavy wheels grinding gravel beneath them. He heard two doors slam closed, and the sound of boots running towards the front door. He tried to move but pins and needles rioted through his body, as frantic as the TV static that threw its light onto his face.

'They're here,' he whispered, as the pounding in the walls suddenly stopped to be replaced by a far more comforting knock on the door.

# ELEVEN

'It was one of those stupid moments when I thought I might like to put down roots.' Jack's hands were moving at great speed, grabbing what to Gwen seemed a random selection of wires and components from the metal shelving. 'They don't happen often, and when they do I stamp on them quick. They cause nothing but trouble.'

'And mortgage payments,' Gwen chipped in, opening the large canvas bag wider so that Jack could drop everything in.

'It seemed a good idea at the time. It was a nice place, and I could afford it.'

'Bit big for a man on his own, perhaps?'

'I like my space,' he replied with a grin. 'Besides, I often had company.'

Jack grabbed what looked like a tape deck and dropped

it into the bag, making Gwen grunt with the weight.

'I just bet you did.' She put the bag down and zipped it shut. 'What's all this stuff for anyway? Shouldn't we be on our way?'

'I'm going as fast as I can!' Jack grabbed another bag. 'But we may need some of this stuff if we're going ghost-hunting.'

'Who ya gonna call?' Gwen muttered, deadpan.

'Torchwood!' Jack yelled, shouldering the second bag. 'To the Mystery Machine!'

'Don't try and quote popular culture,' Gwen sighed. 'You always get it wrong.'

'Never,' Jack laughed, heading out of the Hub. 'I am the man with his finger on the pulse.'

'This from the man who thought *Little Britain* starred Tommy Handley…' Gwen replied, following after him.

Down in the Autopsy Room, Alexander sighed and lifted his head from his examination of Danny Wilkinson's body.

'Excuse me, children!' he shouted. 'May I remind you that some of us are trying to *work* down here?'

He waited for a response, but the only one he got was the heavy Hub door rolling closed behind Jack and Gwen. The penny dropped. 'Oi!' he shouted. 'I'm still down here!' He dropped his scalpel next to Danny's sliced kidneys and pounded his fist on the examination table. 'Bloody *typical*…'

\*\*\*

Gwen often moaned that Jack drove like he did everything in life: aggressively, theatrically and at enough speed that he hoped people wouldn't notice the rough edges. He had never had an accident, but Gwen wasn't sure why not; he seemed to be working very hard at it after all. Ianto had told her about the number of speeding tickets the police sent to the dummy license address – it was a morning's work every few weeks hacking into the system and making them all vanish again.

'I thought there was no such thing as ghosts,' she said, trying to take her mind off the journey.

'There's not…' Jack replied, using the gears to slow him down enough to take a roundabout without sending the SUV into a roll. 'Not in the traditional sense anyway. That doesn't mean there aren't phenomena that have given rise to the *belief* in ghosts over the years.'

'Residual haunting, right? The stuff that Bernie Harris's ghost machine picked up on.'

'Not quite. That machine was a quantum transducer that allowed you to see images outside your own temporal fixed point. That's actually more of a Time TV than a ghost machine.'

'Time TV?' Gwen raised an eyebrow.

Jack smiled. 'Residual haunting is the idea that emotional events of sufficient potency give off a wave of energy that is stored in solid matter – an old house, a murder weapon, a site of historical violence – and are then picked up later like psychic radio and re-experienced by someone sufficiently attuned to those frequencies. It was put forward as a theory in the early 1960s. It's been a popular explanation for ghosts ever since.'

'Popular? Not correct?'

'Not *quite*. Matter and energy just don't work that way. Taking for granted that emotional outbursts can be stored in physical matter – which they *can*, but in a such a weak and fragile form that most dissipate quickly – the human skull exists as an insulator against stray electromagnetic fields bombarding the brain. We'd be freaking out every time someone turned on a mobile phone otherwise.' He shut up for a second, concentrating on avoiding a group of teenagers crossing the road. One of them stuck their middle finger up at him as the drag from the vehicle sent him off balance and into the gutter.

'You missed,' Gwen said.

'Better luck next time.'

'So… skull as an insulator…?'

'Yeah, basically we pick up on the vaguest of emotions: déjà vu, maybe a sense that you're not alone in a room… nothing concrete, nothing *visual*. For that you'd need one hell of an amplifier. Cardiff's sat on one with the Rift, of course, but even then it would take an incredibly focused burst of energy to visualise something without some pretty nifty equipment.'

'But it's possible?'

'Oh *yeah*… and not just in Cardiff. Most hot spots for ghost sightings have some kind of external influence at work – Borley Rectory, the Treasurer's House in York… both the sights of some pretty major temporal fallout. It's not always natural, though. I remember this old museum in Stratford-upon-Avon, built its whole reputation on the amount of supernatural sightings within its walls… The owner was bombarding the place with hallucinogenic theta waves, hoping to summon up Shakespeare. People were tripping their rocks off the minute they crossed the threshold.'

'What did you do?'

'Locked him in his own gift shop for four days. Poor guy was convinced he was Oliver Cromwell by the time I let him out. He's probably back to eating solids by now… *Anyway*…' He turned into Penylan Road. 'The point is: it takes a lot of factors to come together in order to provide an actual physical manifestation, and even then it's worth checking it's not something altogether different…'

They were distracted by the flashing lights of a police car and an ambulance. The woman that Ianto had seen killed earlier was being zipped into a body bag and carried away from the scene.

Jack wound down his window and called to one of the police officers. 'What happened?'

The policeman looked him up and down. 'You lot, is it?' He checked over his shoulder to make sure nobody was listening. 'Looks like hit and run, woman was knocked over coming out of the shop over there, dragged halfway up the road, right state she is. No bugger saw anything, of course, but it doesn't take Quincy to piece it together. Unless you know different?'

Jack smiled. 'Of course not.' He shoved the SUV back

into first gear. 'Just passing by. See you around.'

'Bloody hope not.'

Jack wound the window back up. 'Let's hope that's a coincidence, shall we?'

'Violent death? Coincidence? Us?' Gwen didn't believe it for a moment.

'Ianto's the priority. Everything else can wait.'

Around the corner, Jack swung the SUV off the road and into Jackson Leaves' small forecourt. He was out of the vehicle before Gwen had so much as unclipped her seatbelt. She joined him at the door as he rapped insistently on the wood.

'Can you smell onions?' she asked as they waited for someone to answer. When nobody had after a few seconds, Jack opened the door and stormed inside.

'You don't still own the place, you know,' Gwen said, following awkwardly.

'Now's not the time for formalities,' Jack replied, looking around the hall. 'Hasn't changed much… Hello?' he shouted. 'Mr Wallace? Ianto?'

There was a sound of movement from behind one of the doors and he ran forward, storming into the lounge and narrowly avoiding the poker Rob swung at him as he crossed the threshold.

'Rob Wallace, I presume?' Jack said, pulling the poker from the panicked man's hand and holding up his own in a gesture of surrender. 'The door *was* open…'

# TWELVE

The knocking on the door, coming so soon after the noise that had surrounded them, wasn't the relief to Rob and Julia that it was to Ianto, still barely able to move as he lay on his back in front of the unlit fire.

'What did he say?' Julia asked, looking at Ianto and fully expecting another onslaught of apparitions to attack them.

Rob grabbed the poker from beside the hearth. 'Nothing that makes me feel any better.'

'It's all right…' Ianto whispered, his chattering teeth cutting the words into brittle sounds as they tumbled from his mouth. 'Let them in…'

They heard the sound of the front door opening, and Rob turned to face the lounge door, poker in hand. 'So *you* say…' he whispered, tightening his grip on the brass handle. He was sick of being on the receiving end of the night's many impossibilities.

He heard the intruder shouting his name.

The door opened, and Rob prepared to fight his way past whatever was behind it. The poker was out of his hand before he had even been truly aware of swinging it.

'The door *was* open…' said the intruder.

'I saw you before.' It was Julia, putting her hand on her husband's shoulder as she spoke to the newcomer. 'You were with the police.'

'Sort of,' Gwen stepped into the room. 'We work with them occasionally.'

Jack pushed his way past Rob and Julia, dropping to his haunches by Ianto.

'Hi there, frigid,' he said with a smile.

'Sod off,' Ianto stuttered, 'and get something to warm me up.'

'Now may not be the time or place…' Jack turned to Rob and Julia. 'Got any alcohol?'

'No…' Rob was struggling to maintain any feeling of being in control. 'I was lighting a fire…'

'So light it.'

Rob stepped forward before anger stopped him. 'Look! What's going on here? You say you're with the police?'

'Not as such,' Gwen tried to force her face into the most reassuring shape she could manage, used to being the politician among them. 'We're independent of them. But yes, our paths cross from time to time. Why don't we sit down and go through what happened?'

'I'm not staying here a minute longer,' Julia said.

'We saw a woman appear out of thin air…' Rob shouted. 'Killed herself in the bath… not in our bathroom you understand, no, in the spare *bloody* bedroom…'

'There's a fat man…' Julia added, 'in an old suit… he smells…'

'Banging on the walls, voices in the TV…'

'Your friend, appearing out of nowhere in our airing cupboard…'

'Our bloody *airing cupboard!*'

Their voices were getting louder and louder, blending into one another.

Gwen knew if they carried on she'd never get them under control. 'Please!' she shouted. 'One at a time… We can handle this, but we need to know what's been going on.'

'Handle it on your own,' Rob said, grabbing Julia's hand. 'We're not staying…'

They marched out of the door, and Gwen turned to Jack.

'One thing at a time,' he spat. 'It's not as if I can shoot them. Though it is tempting.'

The walls shook as the front door slammed closed behind the terrified pair.

Jack struck a couple of matches and touched them to the dry newspaper in the hearth. 'All the home comforts…' he muttered, biting his lip as the words brought a memory to mind…

***

*The agent wore his suit as if it were for a wedding or funeral, alien to its woollen threads. Whenever he thought Jack wasn't looking, he pulled at the white collar of his shirt, the starch irritating his skin.*

'All the home comforts, Mister Harkness,' he said. 'Modern fixtures and fittings for both fashion and convenience.'

Jack ran his fingers along the patterns in the Lincrusta wallpaper. 'Yes, it's all very cutting edge.'

'Excuse me?'

'An American expression, probably,' Jack replied, brushing the comment away and also, with his finger, a light covering of dust from the Dado rail.

'Oh,' the agent laughed gushingly. 'Of course! America must be so exciting…'

'Especially if you live in San Francisco,' Jack replied. The agent looked bemused. 'Earthquake trouble,' Jack explained.

'Really? How awful. Mind you, we have the odd tremor here in Cardiff.'

Jack smiled. 'There must be a rift here or something.'

'Do you think so?' The agent looked genuinely concerned by the idea. 'I do hope not…'

'I'll take the risk.' Jack laughed and patted the agent on the arm. 'And the house.'

'Oh!' The agent was quite beside himself, and Jack began to suspect this was his first sale. 'How splendid!'

'Yes,' Jack replied, smiling at the man's enthusiasm. 'One thing though.' He stepped out into the hall. 'Might you be able to have a lock fitted to the study? I'm often involved in rather… delicate work.'

*This made the agent almost purple with excitement. 'Aha! Secret work, is it, sir?' he asked. 'I thought you carried that look about you. One can always tell a man that might be involved in our country's more "specialised" services.' He winked.*

*'One would hope not,' Jack replied.*

*The agent went into a panic. 'Oh… I wasn't meaning to suggest you were in any way deficient in your… ah…'*

*Jack patted him on the shoulder before he had a fit in the hallway. 'Don't worry, I'm not a spy, and I'm pulling your leg. But yes, my work does often involve the safety of the nation. Sometimes even beyond it!'*

*The agent nodded and mopped at his sweating forehead. 'Sir, it is an honour then to assist you.' He tried a smile but he was still too nervous, so it gave the impression he was simply exhibiting teeth. 'Perhaps we should return to the office, where we can begin to make arrangements with your bank…'*

*'Bank?' Jack shrugged. 'I'll just pay cash if that's all right.'*

The fire began to curl around the kindling, a cracking sound like a rifle shot bringing Jack out of his memory.

'Lovely,' Ianto stuttered, his teeth still chattering. 'Now if someone would just fetch me a mug of cocoa and enough brandy to knock out a horse, I'll be right as rain.'

'What happened?' asked Gwen.

'I was out on the street,' Ianto replied, 'grabbing some food and keeping my head down for half an hour.' He tugged the blanket tighter around him. 'There was a chronon surge… huge… and this woman… this is going to sound ridiculous… it was as if she was hit by a tram, except there *was* no tram. I could *hear* it, the wheels on the tracks, the smell of the ozone. I could even sort of feel it, the heaviness of it coming towards me. It hit her square on and sent her flying towards me. Still you couldn't see it, just this mangled woman, bones snapping but with no… reason.' He looked up at Jack and Gwen and rolled his eyes. 'And if you think that's unusual, just wait until the bit where I vanish into thin air and reappear in the airing cupboard upstairs.'

'Covered in ice,' Gwen added.

'Yes…' Ianto shivered. 'I bet things are going to fall off with frostbite.'

'If they do, I'm keeping 'em,' said Jack.

Gwen ignored him. 'What did you see?' she asked Ianto.

'Not much, to be honest. I've been a bit out of it. I heard the pounding on the walls and the TV turning on by itself.'

'Power surge…' Jack commented.

'And the walls?' Gwen asked.

'That'll be the ghosts.' Jack grinned. 'I'm going to take a look around.'

He marched out of the room, pulling the door closed behind him.

For a minute he stood in the hall, listening to Gwen as she told Ianto the history of the building. Around him the beams and joists of Jackson Leaves creaked under the weight of the memories they held for him.

He stroked the off-white banister.

'You need a cleaner,' he said, blowing the dust off his finger.

'What?' Jack asked from the first floor.

'"Pardon",' Alison replied. 'Not "what", you dreadful colonial.'

Jack's head appeared from over the banister above her head. 'Do forgive my lack of breeding, madam,' he joked. 'Might I enquire as to what it was that you said previously? My dull foreign ears struggled to catch your regal tone.'

'I said you needed a cleaner, the banister is filthy.'

'Just like its owner, then,' Jack replied.

She sighed but couldn't hide the smile on her lips. 'There's no hope for you.'

'Agreed, none whatsoever. So, do you like the house?'

'It could be lovely,' she replied, 'with a woman's touch.'

Jack smiled down at her. 'I say again: just like its owner, then.'

'Anyone's touch will suffice for him,' she replied, an air of sadness to her voice.

'But your touch is the sweetest.'

She joined him on the landing. 'So you say today,' she replied, 'but who will it be tomorrow?'

He took her in his arms. 'Stay the night and find out.'

She shivered in his embrace.

'You all right?' he asked.

She nodded. 'It felt like something touched me.'

'Give me a few moments and it certainly will,' he grinned.

She slapped his arm playfully. 'Really…' She looked around and then, seeing nothing, tried to dismiss her feeling of unease. She smiled. 'Perhaps you've got ghosts…'

'Too many to mention, but don't worry, I won't let them have you!' He lifted her off the floor and carried her towards the bedroom.

On the landing, Jack paused to breathe in the stale air… trying to remember the scent of Alison's perfume, of her skin.

Off the landing, the first room confused him. Where he had expected to see the bath, he found instead a tatty single bed and a brown carpet that he would have burned on principle had he had a match on him.

'Look at the state of you,' he whispered.

'Look at the state of you,' Miles said, running the sponge across Jack's shoulders. The soapy water making gritty, brown rivers of the dried mud on his back.

'I slipped,' Jack replied.

'Clearly… but what would the neighbours think,' Miles asked, 'had they happened to glance out of their window to see a naked man thrashing around in the mud.'

'They'd probably ask me to bring them some coal, too, save them going out in the rain.'

'You could have put some clothes on!'

Jack winked over his shoulder. 'I'd only have had to take them off again.' He reached over the side of the bath for the brandy bottle. 'Another drink?'

Miles shook his head. 'I'm away with the fairies as it is.'

Jack grinned and leaned over to kiss him. 'Indeed you are.'

***

THE HOUSE THAT JACK BUILT

The next room was still the main bedroom. Jack stepped inside, lifted up the collapsed, part-constructed wardrobe and leaned it against the wall. The bed was built but not made, just a bare mattress…

*'You buy a house with cash and then seem unable to afford a bed,'* Alison sighed, lying back on the mattress that lay in the middle of the room.

*'I just keep forgetting,'* Jack replied, rolling onto his front. He blew on her chest and chuckled as her nipple hardened in the cool air. *'Beds are for sleeping, and I don't do much of that.'*

*'I noticed,'* she replied, not unkindly. She twisted to kiss him on the forehead and grabbed the blanket to wrap around herself. *'I'm going to marry him, you know.'*

*Jack propped himself up on his elbow. 'I know.'*

*'He loves me very much, and he's a good man.'*

*'I've never said otherwise.'*

*She threw him a glance. 'It's not like I have other offers.'*

*Jack nodded but didn't reply. He'd had that conversation too many times over the years and wasn't inclined to have it with Alison as well. If this was coming to an end – and it looked as if that was the case – then let it at least do so with some grace.*

*'I'm sure he can make you happy,' he said instead.*

*She stared at him. 'No you're not, and neither am I. But happiness is overrated. Sometimes you just have to settle for contentment.'*

'Story of my life,' Jack said, stepping out of the bedroom and back onto the landing.

The bathroom was new, well, no… new to *Jack* but it could hardly be called new otherwise. It was a cheap suite with oyster-shell soap trays and a colour of yellow one could never have found outside a plastics factory. Little blue fish swam in circles on the tiles. It was ghastly.

Jack walked back out and made his way up to the second floor.

At the top of the stairs the landing offered two choices, a room to either side.

*'What do you need so many rooms for, anyway?' Miles asked, gazing out of the window at the leafy trees of the road below.*

*Jack watched the muscles in Miles's legs and buttocks tighten as the man went on tiptoes. 'I like variety,' he replied, taking a sip of his drink. 'A room for every occasion.'*

*'Or guest?' Miles asked, turning around and treating Jack to a change of scenery.*

*'Sometimes,' Jack admitted. 'That bother you?'*

*'No. Why should it? I know the rules of our affaire.' Miles topped up his own glass from the decanter on the sideboard. He took a big mouthful. 'I'm going to marry her,' he said, and was then perplexed as to why this should cause so much hilarity in Jack. 'I'm glad my life amuses you so,' he said with some bite.*

*'It's not your life I was finding amusing,' Jack replied. 'It was mine.'*

Both rooms were empty and in a much worse state than the rest of the house. It looked like nobody had been up here for years. A fat wolf spider hid in the corner of the

114

skirting board, draped coyly in sheets of its web. Jack prodded at it with his boot but it refused to run, clinging to the paint-chipped wood with utter determination.

'To have and to hold…'

'… in sickness and in health…'

Jack tried to stifle a yawn. Church ceremonies bored him. Weddings were a poor excuse for distant family and even more distant friends to get together and bitch about a marriage that probably wouldn't last. As far as he was concerned, you could do that much easier in a bar, with the added bonus that some drunken old duffer in a frock wouldn't feel the need to keep bringing God into it.

'Heavenly father…' whined the priest, who was certainly as old – and if the volume of his proclamations was anything to go by – as deaf as the deity he worshipped, 'by your blessing let these rings be to Miles and Alison a symbol of unending love and faithfulness…'

Now there, thought Jack, is your problem already. Why set these poor kids up to fail before they've even got the rings on?

Alison looked towards the congregation and glimpsed Jack at the back. He gave what he hoped was a supportive smile, but maybe it didn't come out too well as she didn't look happy to see him. When she looked back at her husband-to-be, Miles caught the flicker of concern in her gaze. His brow furrowed slightly, perhaps worried that she was having second thoughts.

'… through Jesus Christ our Lord, Amen.'

The amen rippled through the crowd, and Miles also noticed

Jack. His response was, if anything, worse than Alison's. The sudden flash of panicked guilt that ran across his face was plain, and Jack realised he shouldn't have come.

'The rings?' asked the priest.

'Er…' Miles stammered. 'Yes… sorry…' He took the ring from his best man and placed it rather nervously on Alison's finger.

The priest continued intoning the words to the service: 'I give you this ring as a sign of our marriage.'

Miles repeated them. 'I give you this ring as a sign of our marriage.'

'With my body I honour you…'

'With my b… body I honour you…' A thin sheen of sweat was beginning to blossom on his forehead.

Alison, seeing his discomfort, had clearly assumed the worst. Somehow he must know about her and Jack. She too began to tremble, which only fuelled Miles's panic. How could he have trusted Jack not to tell Alison about their affaire? Would Alison tell? His reputation would be ruined…

As they continued to repeat the words of the service, becoming more and more visibly concerned, a faint mumble began to build throughout the congregation. What was wrong? Was it just nerves? Was one of them going to back out?

Jack winced at the discomfort of it all. The mood in the church worsened by the second and, when he couldn't take it a moment longer, he began to make his way out of the back door. He shouldn't have come in the first place. The least he could do was ensure he made himself scarce now.

As he stepped out into the fresh air, taking deep lungfuls of it in relief, the priest's voice followed him:

'Those whom God has joined together, let no man put asunder.'

Jack stepped into the other room, a train of dusty spider's web dragging behind him. It was just as dilapidated, the paintwork peeling, the wood flaking.

Jack looked out of the window, the arcs of the streetlights pulled into contortions by the heavy rain beating against the glass. His own reflection looked back at him, and he realised he was crying. This surprised him…

*…he wasn't a man prone to tears but he felt them now. Whether they were through sadness or guilt he couldn't rightfully say. Looking down on Alison's pale-blue face, her hair plastered against her head with dirty river water he didn't see anything of the beautiful woman he had known. He couldn't imagine having kissed those wrinkled cheeks, those puffy lips. The Alison he had known was long gone.*

*'Not married more than twenty-four hours,' said the police inspector. 'Husband drowns her and then – when the prissy little sod can't take the guilt of it – comes running to us. Says it was to protect his reputation, would you believe? Not worth much now, is it? Murdering bastard. Nothing strange to it though… oh…'scuse me…'*

*The inspector hawked phlegm into a yellow handkerchief and rubbed at his bushy moustache.*

*'Touch of the vapours, isn't it? As I was saying, seems perfectly straightforward, not the sort of thing you lot need to poke your*

*nose into. Don't know why anyone called you, frankly. Not much you can do for her, is there?'*

'No,' Jack replied, 'not any more.'

Jack rubbed at his eyes, left the room and went down the stairs to check his face in the bathroom mirror. He was damned if he was going to let Gwen and Ianto see he'd been crying. Hadn't he been thinking earlier how he couldn't afford to get caught up in his memories? They were no use to him, nothing but dead weight that would drag him down if he let them.

He grinned at the mirror, looking fine, and went back out onto the landing. A flash of movement caught his eye, something red in the shadows of the main bedroom. He looked around. Nothing there.

As he descended the stairs, the front door opened and Rob and Julia walked back in.

'Changed your mind?' Jack asked as Julia slammed the front door closed behind her.

'Impossible...' Rob muttered, sliding down the wall and sitting on the floor, leaving a snail-trail of rainwater behind him on the paintwork. *'Impossible.'*

'What is?' Jack asked.

'What's going on?' Gwen asked, stepping out of the lounge.

'It's gone...' Julia said.

'Gone?' said Jack.

Julia gestured beyond the front door. 'Out there... It's all... It's *gone.'*

Jack pushed past her and reached for the door handle.

'You don't want to go out there,' Julia said.

'I do,' he replied, the words bringing his memories back to him as he pulled the door open and stepped out onto the front step. The rain was still just as heavy, and he pulled up the collar of his coat as he walked out across the gravel, past the SUV and to the mouth of the drive. The street beyond had vanished, nothing but a wall of darkness filling the driveway.

He held his hand out in front of him and moved forward. As his toes drew close to the pavement, his hand suddenly felt numb. Staring at it, he gave an impressed whistle as it appeared to fade out of sight. Pulling it back, there was a resistance to the air but his hand was returned to him.

'What is it?'

Jack turned to see Gwen. 'No idea,' he admitted. 'But for now I'd say we're stuck here, wouldn't you?'

# THIRTEEN

'The door *was* open,' the strange man said, holding his hands out in front of him as if Rob were no danger at all. That was already a lie, though, as far as Rob was concerned, rubbing his wrist where it had been twisted when the poker was wrenched from his grip. A dark-haired woman followed the man into the room, offering an apologetic look that didn't wash for one minute.

'I saw you before,' Julia said to the man, confusing Rob even further. What was she talking about? They'd never clapped eyes on him, he was sure of that. 'You were with the police,' she continued.

'Sort of,' said the woman. The American ignored both of them, pushing his way past and talking to the man that had appeared upstairs. 'We work with them occasionally,' the woman continued.

*What's that supposed to mean?* Rob thought, only too aware he was being fobbed off. His heart was pounding in his chest… what was going on? God, but he needed a drink.

'Got any alcohol?' said the American, as if he'd been reading his mind.

'No…' Rob was wrong-footed. What did this guy think this was? A house-party? Oh… alcohol… the penny dropped…for the man… to warm him up. It wasn't as if they hadn't been looking after him. 'I was lighting a fire…'

'So light it.'

Rob found he was actually stepping forward for a second before he stopped himself. 'Look! What's going on here?' he shouted, sick of being on the receiving end. 'You say you're with the police?'

'Not as such.' The woman again; the bloody man was never going to answer his questions it would seem. 'We're independent of them,' she continued. 'But yes, our paths cross from time to time. Why don't we sit down and go through what happened?'

Julia shook her head. 'I'm not staying here a minute longer.'

Rob's head hurt with the confusion of it all. He tried to put it into words: 'We saw a woman appear out of thin air… Killed herself in the bath… Not in our bathroom, you understand, no, in the spare *bloody* bedroom…'

'There's a fat man…' Julia added, 'in an old suit… he smells…'

'Banging on the walls, voices in the TV…'

'Your friend, appearing out of nowhere in our airing cupboard…'

'Our bloody *airing cupboard*!'

It was uncontrollable now, the words falling from him like vomit, poison that needed to be ejected. Dear Lord, but what was he going to do? He wasn't sure he could handle this… Everything felt hazy…

'Please!' the woman shouted. 'One at a time… We can handle this, but we need to know what's been going on.'

There was only one thing Rob could think to do. 'Handle it on your own,' he said, grabbing his wife's hand. 'We're not staying…'

It didn't occur to him to question leaving them in the house; at that moment, they were welcome to it. He needed to get out, needed to clear his head. Another moment stuck in there and he honestly thought he might lose his mind.

He checked his jeans pocket, giving a sigh of relief as he felt the reassuring shape of his van keys. That was all they needed. In a couple of minutes, they'd be driving down the road, heading as far away as they could.

'Come on,' he said to Julia, pushing her out of the door in front of him. 'The flat's empty for another week yet, we can stay there.'

The rain was still lashing down and neither of them was wearing a coat. They were soaked through in moments, but they didn't care.

Rob stared at the American's big black car. 'Typical

yank, that is,' he commented, pulling Julia around it by her arm. 'Compensation for something else.'

His anger was hardening into a lump in his throat, his teeth grinding as he fought to stop himself kicking at the stupid bloody car until he did some damage. Fear had set him off now and he was finding it hard to keep himself straight, his muscles twitching and pulsing, his head swimming with it... he wanted to kick and punch and scrape and tear...

'Rob!' Julia's voice, thin and whining, *damn her*.

'I told you, it'll be fine,' he said, rubbing the rainwater from his face. Couldn't she tell that he was struggling? He didn't need her wheedling at him.

'Hurting...' she said, and he turned on her, fist clenching, only to freeze as he saw the bright white dimples in her arm where he was digging his fingers in as hard as he could. The ragged edge of one of his nails had drawn blood.

Suddenly it was gone, all of it, the huge pressure that he had fought to keep in, vanished in an instant. He let go of her arm and put his hand to his mouth.

'I'm sorry,' he whispered. 'I didn't realise.'

She was scared. She had that same look in her eyes that she'd had when he'd hit her a few months ago. He hadn't meant to, now or then. Sometimes he just got so angry, it was horrible... To feel such uncontrollable rage, to be shaking with it, to need to thrash and hit just to shake the feeling out of his muscles, the feeling that he was going to rupture.

She had nearly left him, he knew that; he'd scared her enough. The terrible thing was that he hadn't even *wanted* to hit her – he'd caught her by accident. But the look she'd given him when the back of his hand had hit her temple… It was so full of disgust at him… such contempt… He had hit her again, just to earn it.

'Please, I wouldn't have…' There was a look of disbelief in her eyes now and he found himself almost wishing her to push it. He hadn't been directing any of his anger at her – wouldn't have done – but after everything that had happened tonight, wasn't he allowed to lose it a little? The look on her face said not, and that was nearly enough to set him off again. Nearly.

He held up his hands placatingly. 'I wasn't angry at you, sweetheart, just freaked out, you know? I told you before, that was just… I don't know what that was… but I'd never do it again, OK?' He tried to look friendly, tried to soften his eyes. 'I couldn't hurt you, babe, never…' He held out his hands to her. 'Please? Forgive me? Let's get out of here, OK? Go where it's safe.'

After a moment, she nodded and took his hands.

He gave her a genuine smile then and pulled the van keys from his pocket. 'So sorry, baby,' he said. 'I just lost it in there, what with everything, you know?'

'I know.'

They hunched over in the rain and started to walk quickly up the road.

'What do you think it was?' he asked.

'I don't know.' Relief, both at being out of the building

and having Rob calm down, had begun to squeeze tears out of the corners of her eyes, and she rubbed them away with the rainwater. 'I don't believe in…'

'Ghosts and stuff?'

'Yeah. Mum always used to. She loved it, always reading books about it… but, well… I thought it was rubbish.'

'Same here. Good at the movies but don't believe a word of it at home.'

'So there must be a scientific explanation?'

'To the fact that we both saw a woman kill herself in the bedroom and a man appear in the airing cupboard?'

They looked at one another and burst out laughing. There was as much panic in it as humour, in fact they could just as easily have been screaming, but it helped for the moment, a release of the pressure that had been building all night. Rob hugged Julia and they carried on walking, his arm around her shoulders.

'It'll be all right,' he said. 'It'll seem better in the morning.'

'Where did you park the van?' Julia asked, though she knew the answer, had seen him park it there earlier when the police had cordoned off the road.

'It's there,' he said, pointing at the white van just along the road, 'just a few doors up.'

'So how come it's taking us so long?' Julia asked, that note of panic returning to her voice.

'It's not. I mean, we only just left…'

They were stood outside Jackson Leaves. They hadn't moved an inch.

'But that's ridiculous…' muttered Rob. 'We walked all the way up…' He looked ahead of them, and they started to walk again, the hedge moving past them, the parked cars.

'It's fine,' he said. 'I don't know what happened, but look, the van's just there.' He pointed at it with the keys. Only a few houses away. They kept walking… and walking… and walking…

Julia gripped Rob's arm even tighter as she turned to look up at Jackson Leaves, the tatty gables, the loose guttering that dripped in this constant damn rain…

'It won't let us go!' she cried.

'It's just a house,' Rob said, pulling her – gentler this time – along the pavement. 'It's just bricks and rot and damp…'

They began to run. Rob kept his eyes fixed on the van, pointing the keys at it like a talisman as they ran faster and faster towards it. The rain made it hard, stinging in his eyes and making his feet slip on the pavement, but he focused hard and pushed forward… They'd make it…

His feet lost their grip in the wet and he fell, pulling Julia down with him. They landed on the pavement with a grunt, Rob jarring his elbow on the tarmac and Julia scraping her side.

'Stupid…' he rubbed at his elbow. 'Sorry, love, clumsy idiot.'

Julia wasn't listening. She was looking up at Jackson Leaves.

It was staring right back.

127

'I don't get it,' he said. 'This is stupid. We *were* moving, you could tell we were…' He looked along the road towards the van. 'Everything was moving but we weren't getting any closer to the things further away. Which doesn't make sense.'

'None of it does, and none of it will,' Julia said quietly. 'It just *is*. We should go back inside.'

'No way,' Rob said, getting to his feet. 'I'm not setting one foot back in that house, we're getting out of here if it ki—'

'Don't say that,' Julia interrupted. 'Don't encourage it.'

Rob put his hands on her cheeks, rubbing the rain from her eyes with his thumbs. 'Come on, babe,' he said. 'Keep it together, and we'll get out of here, OK?'

She got to her feet but made no sign of agreeing with him.

'We'll try the other way,' he said. 'Walk down to the high street.'

He turned her away from the house, doing his best not to look at it himself, and they began to walk along the pavement in the other direction.

'It'll be fine,' he said. 'You'll see. In a minute, all of this is just going to stop and we'll be back to normal. We'll probably even laugh about it, that stupid night when we got ourselves all turned around until we didn't know what was happening… Shared hysteria, that's what it is… Derren Brown stuff.' He scuffed at the puddles beneath their feet, sending a spray of rainwater into the darkness ahead of them as if to test whether it was safe. 'We won't be able to figure out how we got so wound up, just you watch, it'll be that night that we lost it,' he laughed. 'That night we went so bloody mad we ended up walking around in the rain while some American nutjob tried to burgle us. That's it, you know,' he continued, moving a little faster. 'That whole thing in there was just some kind of trick so that they could get in the place and turn it over. Not that they'll find anything worth having, not in that stupid… bastard… *house!*' This last was screamed at Jackson Leaves, still stood, uncaring, to the side of them.

'I don't know,' he said, dropping down to sit on the kerb. 'I just don't know.'

After a moment she sat down next to him. 'We'll have to go back inside,' she said.

He shook his head. 'I'm not going back in there.'

'It's no better out here.' She had become gentle, only too aware of how close Rob was to breaking. He wasn't violent any more, he was too scared even for that. You couldn't fight Jackson Leaves.

'I just can't bear the idea of going back in there, baby,' he said, starting to cry. 'That noise, the blood and water… I just can't…'

'We have to,' she replied. 'Look at it out here, it's just as wrong. Look at the rain.' She held out her hand and swiped it gently from right to left in front of his eyes, and for the first time he noticed that the rain wasn't moving. Droplets were stationary in the air. He suddenly realised the rain was silent around them. Looking back over his shoulder towards the house, the rain there was splashing down on the plants, the roof tiles, that stupid American's car. But here? Stillness…

'How is that even possible?' he asked, sticking out his hand and touching the droplets with his fingers, watching as the glistening balls, fat with the stolen light from street lamps, popped against his touch.

'I'm sure there's a proper scientific explanation,' said Julia with a half-smile. She looked up at Jackson Leaves, noticing movement at the upstairs windows. Right on the top floor, the wide shoulders of the American filled one of the window frames as he stared out into the night, though whether it was the night *she* stood in she couldn't say. Something told her not; that there was more of a gap between them than simply the hedge and driveway. Directly beneath him, one floor down, a blob of red paisley alerted her to the fat man's presence. Unlike the American, she knew that he *was* watching her and Rob, and whatever version of the world this was that had trapped them was one that the fat man knew well. *He* could move along these pavements and roads, of that she had no doubt.

'It's…' Rob was staring along the road into the distance. 'I don't know, something's happening.'

Julia followed his gaze and tried to figure out what he was seeing. There was certainly something wrong, but it was hard to put your finger on. 'We need to move,' she said, as it became clear. 'We need to move *now*, Rob, while we still can.'

He stared along the street, watching as one by one the

cars and houses in the distance disappeared. A great wave of darkness was sweeping towards them, swallowing each droplet of rain, each inch of pavement and road. Who knew what would happen if they were still sat there when it arrived? Julia was right, there wasn't good enough cause to find out.

He got to his feet and they moved towards Jackson Leaves, the sound of the rain in front of them building with every step. He took one look over his shoulder just before crossing the threshold, the darkness was nearly on them, it had taken the houses, the trees, it had even taken his van.

'Come on, then,' he said, and they walked into the moving curtain of rain that would lead them back home.

# FOURTEEN

Gwen was getting all motherly, tugging the blanket tighter around Ianto as he shivered. 'What did you see?' she asked him.

'Not much to be honest,' he admitted, staring at the fire Jack had just lit and willing it to get going. If it didn't get a good blaze on within five minutes, he'd start shoving furniture in the grate, he was *so* cold. 'I've been a bit out of it. I heard the pounding on the walls though, and the TV turned on by itself.'

'Power surge...' said Jack in a casual manner that didn't convince Ianto for one moment.

It didn't convince Gwen either. 'And the walls?'

'That'll be the ghosts,' was Jack's dismissive reply. 'I'm going to take a look around,' he said with a grin, changing the subject before either could ask any more questions.

In case they tried anyway, he strolled out of the room.

'That's our Jack,' Ianto muttered. 'Quick with the knob gags and melodrama but light on cold, hard facts.'

'You know what he's like,' Gwen said, putting some more dry wood on the fire.

'Don't I just.'

'There's certainly a lot more to this place than meets the eye,' Gwen said, pulling her PDA out of her jacket pocket, opening up some of the files on the house that she had ported across and handing it to Ianto. 'The history of the building is a tabloid's dream: suicides, murders… and you'll never believe who the first person to own it was.'

'Jack.'

Gwen swore under her breath. 'Fine, make me look an idiot. Everyone knew but me.'

'Sorry. But there's not much about him that I don't know.' Ianto stood up and moved over to the rug directly in front of the fire. 'Actually, that's not true,' he continued, sitting on the rug and holding his hands out towards the flames. 'I doubt I know a fraction of what's worth knowing, but what little of his life is on file I've found it, read it…' he looked up at her and gave an embarrassed smile, 'learnt it. I'm like a stupid teenager swotting up with a copy of *Smash Hits*.'

Gwen rested a hand on his shoulder. 'You do know that he's…'

'Just a shag?' Ianto nodded. 'Yes I know. I can't help it though, I've never been much good at casual.' He looked up at her. 'Don't tell him. I don't want to look stupid.'

She squatted down and gave him a peck on the cheek. 'I won't, you're not stupid either, just...'

'Deluded?'

She smiled. 'Yeah, that sounds about right.'

'You wouldn't believe how many places he's lived,' Ianto said. 'That's why I didn't mention it. I assumed it was just a coincidence. He's had places all over Cardiff. Lots of them under false names of course, Robert Gossage, Alan Jones, John Smith... But I've followed the chain of sales. He keeps buying places then selling them on.'

'So he watches *Property Ladder*.'

'It's not that. You know what he's like, he's not interested in money. He's obsessed with trying to find a home, that's what I think.'

'Maybe.' Gwen looked sadly at Ianto. He really had fallen for Jack, hadn't he? 'He did right to sell this place on though,' she said. 'Look at the news reports.'

Ianto got the hint, nodding and reading the small screen in front of him. 'So the question is: did this place turn its residents mad, or are we stood in a psycho magnet?'

'Now there's a lovely thought,' Gwen admitted. 'Perhaps it's just as well the owners did a bunk.'

'They weren't so bad,' Ianto said. 'Just scared. Can't say I blame them either. Still, they tried to look after me, even with everything else going on.' He smiled, the warmth finally creeping back into him. 'That makes them a decent couple in my book. I may send them a Christmas card.'

'"Season's Greetings from the nutter in your airing cupboard"?'

'That sort of thing.'

'Do you remember anything?' Gwen asked. 'Between disappearing on the high street and reappearing here?'

Ianto's face lost some of its humour. 'It was strange… Like a hypnic jerk.'

'A what?'

'That feeling you get when you're just about to fall asleep and your body jolts as if you've fallen or tripped.'

'Oh…' Gwen rolled her eyes. '*That.* You're the first person I've met that wouldn't just call it "that jerky sleep thing".'

'I read books,' Ianto joked. 'Get over it. Anyway, it was like that, a jolt through my body, this feeling of being somewhere else… Nothing specific, just a sense of having moved.' An uncomfortable look passed across his face. 'It scrambled my head. I didn't really know what was happening… It felt like there was something else there.'

'Something or someone?'

'Someone.' He shrugged. 'Like I say, though, it shook me up. Who knows what was going on, eh? Next thing I know, I'm waking up on the floor over there with the whole house going mental.'

'Due to a "power surge".'

Ianto chuckled. 'Could have been worse. He could have said subsidence.'

Gwen nodded. 'When Jack starts talking like a cover story, you know you're in trouble.'

They heard the front door open and exchanged surprised looks. They heard Jack's voice from the stairs.

'Changed your mind?' Neither Gwen nor Ianto could hear the reply, but they recognised Rob's voice.

'I didn't think we'd be seeing them again,' said Gwen, heading out into the hallway.

Ianto listened as Rob and Julia talked about the outside world having 'gone'. The front door opened again as Jack stepped outside. Ianto considered going out after him but decided against it. The fire was just starting to warm him, and a night of impossibilities was beginning to make him jaded. The outside world has vanished? Yes, of course it has, bound to happen…

After a few moments, Jack walked back into the lounge followed by Gwen.

'You feeling any better?' he asked Ianto.

'I'm *feeling*… Frankly, that's an improvement.'

'Good.'

Rob and Julia walked in. Cowed by whatever they had seen outside, there was little argument left in either of them.

'OK,' said Jack. 'For now we're stuck in this place, so let's make the most of it – drag the equipment in, get set up and start trying to find out what's going on.' He turned to Rob and Julia. 'I know this is freaking you both out, but I'm going to need you to keep it together and help me out here, OK?'

'Do we have a choice?' asked Julia.

'Yes,' Jack replied. 'I could drug you and throw you in the boot of the car.'

'Jack,' Gwen hissed.

'What?' Jack replied with a laugh. 'It's a choice!' His smile vanished as he stared at Rob and Julia. 'Believe me, I'll do it for your safety and ours if it looks like the best option.'

'We should always let him deal with the civilians,' Ianto said. 'He's just so good at it.' He got up and started stamping the circulation back into his feet. 'I know it might not seem like it,' he said to Rob and Julia, 'but right now we're the best chance you've got of seeing it through the night.'

'That supposed to make me feel better?' asked Rob.

'If you knew how many times we've probably saved your life already over the years it would,' Jack chipped in. 'This is what we do. Now let us get on and do it.'

Rob held up his hands in surrender. 'Fine…'

'OK,' said Jack. 'We need space and security.'

He walked out of the lounge and headed to the next door along the hall.

'If I remember right, the study has a… aha!' He pointed to the lock in the old door. 'Got the key for this?'

'In the kitchen,' Julia said, walking past him to get it. 'But it's a dining room not a study.'

'Oh, nobody has studies any more,' Jack said sadly, walking in and pulling the cheap pine table over to the far wall. Rob grabbed the chairs, as always happier to be distracted by doing something. An old-fashioned sideboard filled with Julia's aunt's dinner service and some ugly brown glass trifle bowls was left where it was.

Julia came in and handed Jack the key.

'What good's that going to do?' asked Rob.

'You're the one who was hiding in the lounge earlier swinging pokers at people,' Jack retorted, dropping the key into his pocket. 'The night is yet young, who knows how it'll end up?'

He turned to look out of the French windows that filled the far wall. 'This is new.'

'How do you know?' Julia asked, a little ashamed that she couldn't say whether he was right or not.

'I used to live here,' he said. 'Long time ago.'

'It must have been,' Julia replied. 'Auntie Joan was here for… I don't know, thirty years.'

Jack smiled. 'I'm older than I look.'

'He works out,' Ianto said from the doorway. 'What are we bringing in?'

'You stay by the fire for now,' Jack said. 'We can manage.'

'I'd rather get moving, get the circulation flowing.'

Jack grinned. 'I'd love to help but I'm kinda busy!'

'Story of my life.'

'There's a couple of big canvas bags. We'll need as many monitors as we can strip out, all the audio/visual stuff you can get your hands on, basically. We want this place wired for sound.'

'"Power from the needle to the plastic",' Ianto replied, straight-faced, and walked out.

Jack stared after him. 'Please tell me he didn't just quote Cliff Richard at me… He's *so* dumped if he did.'

\*\*\*

Ianto's arms and legs were throbbing, bursts of pins and needles erupting all over as he stepped outside the front door. It was still raining. 'Oh God,' he sighed, 'here's me, about to get hypothermia.'

He ran to the SUV, opened the back door and climbed inside as quickly as possible. Sitting down in the back section, surrounded by the monitoring equipment, he shook some of the water from his hair and worked out what he could take apart without breaking anything. Realising he was missing a trick, he pulled his set of keys out of his pocket and reached forward to turn on the engine and heater. 'Ah…' he sighed as air began to pump out of the vents, 'I may just stay here all night.'

'If you do, so am I,' Gwen said, climbing in.

'Sorry,' Ianto grinned, 'but I've baggsied electrics.' He pulled a toolkit out of the glovebox. 'You carry the bags.'

'I hate you,' Gwen told him, grabbing one of the bags.

'May it keep you as warm as these heaters do me,' Ianto replied. 'Close the door, you're letting in a draft.'

Chuckling as Gwen ran back towards the house, he pulled one of the monitors forward and began to disconnect its cabling.

Gwen nearly slipped on the polished wood of the hall floor but managed to regain her balance by grabbing hold of the banister.

'Careful,' Jack said from the dining room doorway, 'we wouldn't want you falling over and damaging the equipment.'

'I am so going to smack someone this evening,' she said, shoving the bag at him.

Rob watched Jack unpack reams of cabling from the large bag before deciding to leave him to it. The man had made it perfectly clear that his and Julia's input was far from necessary. Arrogant bastard. Rob was beginning to wish he had never called him. The minute all of this strange stuff had started, he and Julia should have been out of the house and away. He bet they would have been fine if they hadn't hung around to help the American's prissy boyfriend.

He went into the kitchen, unsure of what to do with himself but determined to find something to occupy him. He thought about putting the kettle on but decided against it; they'd only ask him to make them a drink as well, and he was neither brave enough to refuse them nor gracious enough to do it. He didn't want to be their slave.

He started poking through the cupboards aimlessly, straightening tins and cartons, ordering things a little more. He opened drawers, altering the order of the cutlery (it went fork, knife, then spoon, *obviously*... that was, after all, the order in which you needed them at the dining table, and why were the forks and spoons not nestling inside one another? It saved on space and looked much neater). He refolded tea towels, matching corner to corner. He turned the glasses so that they rested on their brims (why would you do it any other way? Did you want

141

them to fill with dust?). He caught his reflection in the window, tongue poking out of the corner of his mouth in utter concentration, and it drew him to a halt. What was he doing? He didn't care about this sort of thing normally. Why did it suddenly seem so vital now?

He hugged himself, the sudden urge to cry building in his belly.

What was *wrong* with him?

Julia wanted to be where it was busiest, standing in the corner of the dining room watching Jack as he uncurled wires and stacked cases of equipment on the table.

'Help me out with this?' he asked.

'Sure.'

'Cool.' He held up a deep tray of components, miniature video cameras and microphones. 'I need to get these up all over the place, and if you help out I'll tell you all about ghosts and why they don't exist. Fair deal?'

She smiled and nodded. 'Sounds good to me.'

'OK.' He handed her the tray while he grabbed gaffer tape and as much cabling as he could carry. 'We'll start at the top and work our way down.'

He marched out of the door with Julia following.

'So…' he began. 'Ghosts… The majority of all supernatural phenomena are easily attributed to something else. We are so attuned to the fiction of spooks and haunting that we leap on it as soon as we see something strange. You see, our brains are built to demand explanation and they'll always opt for the most familiar thing they find, in the belief that familiarity equals likelihood.'

Julia was having to jog slightly to keep up with him as he bounded along the first-floor landing and up the next flight of stairs. 'But we actually saw a woman commit suicide. It was hazy but clear – it was *real*. It wasn't something we mistook for a woman in a bath; it *was* a woman in a bath.'

'OK,' Jack replied. 'But that doesn't make it a ghost.'

'What makes you so sure?'

They'd reached the top floor and Jack turned to face her. 'Because I know there's no such thing. I've been dead, and there was nothing there. The only soul I've got was given me by Nina Simone.'

'You've *been* dead?'

'Oh yeah.' Jack poked around in the tray Julia was carrying, picking out a small camera. 'And now I'm walking around. Doesn't make me a ghost though, does it?'

'What was it?' Julia asked. 'Like a near-death experience or something?'

'As near as you can get. I *died* Julia, vaporised, ceased to exist. But something – and no it wasn't supernatural – brought me back. Weird stuff happens – and believe me my life has got weirder since – but there will always be an explanation for it somewhere.' He fixed the camera to the roof with gaffer tape, coiled the video cable and dropped it down the gap between the banisters. 'You read any Arthur C. Clarke?'

'Used to watch his programme with my mum, *Mysterious World* or whatever it was called.'

'There was a lot more to Arthur than that,' Jack said with a smile. 'I shared some wonderful summers with him in Colombo.'

'Of course you did,' Julia replied dismissively.

Jack grinned, not caring in the least whether she believed him or not. He grabbed another camera and walked into one of the empty rooms. 'He wrote three "laws" over the years, the third of which is probably the most famous, though the others are just as accurate.' He fixed the second camera in place in the far corner and trailed the cable back out of the room with them, dropping it again down towards the ground floor. 'He said that "any sufficiently advanced technology is indistinguishable from magic".'

'I've heard that,' Julia admitted as they walked into the next room.

'Yeah, I find myself saying it a lot in this job. That's the problem with the clever things people say, they get quoted so often people forget to pay attention. Think about it, imagine everything we take for granted today and how miraculous it would have seemed a couple of centuries ago. We're always getting closer to understanding, *always*. Ghosts? Visions? They're unexplained today, but tomorrow they'll be science.'

A third camera in place, they began to head down the stairs again.

'OK,' said Julia. 'I accept the idea that we may have

explanations for weird stuff in years to come, but help me out, what could it have been that we saw? It was so real.'

'It was in here, yes?' Jack walked into the spare bedroom.

'Yes.' Julia was embarrassed at how scared she felt walking back into the room, her heart beating faster in her chest and her breath becoming laboured. 'She was right there,' she said, pointing to the bed.

'Which is exactly where the bath used to be,' Jack said. 'When I lived here this was the bathroom. I imagine your aunt changed it after what happened in here.'

'What happened?'

'Your aunt used to keep lodgers, do you remember them?'

That feeling of guilt again. 'I didn't really know her that well. We didn't visit much when I was a kid. You know how it can be with family, you go your separate ways.'

Jack nodded. 'Know what you mean. Well, it doesn't matter. She had lodgers. It helped pay the bills, I guess, stopped her rattling around the place. But… something bad happened to both of them. One, a librarian called Kerry Robinson, slit her wrists in the bath. Right there,' he pointed at the bed.

'So what I saw was just the past? I was watching something that had happened years ago?'

'Exactly. No ghosts, no spirits, just history becoming visible somehow.'

'But how's that possible?'

'That's what we need to find out.'

'But it wasn't a ghost?'

'No.'

'Just an image?'

Jack grinned, fixing a camera in the roof. 'You got it!'

'So when I keep seeing that fat man, he's just an image too?' Julia was beginning to stutter and shake. Jack hadn't realised she'd been this close to breaking, had thought she was getting it together. He never had been much good at reading people.

'It's OK,' he said. 'That's my point, nothing here can harm you. It's just images, that's all, like watching old movie footage. It has no physical presence.'

'But… Rob got wet.'

'What?'

'He tried to help her, the woman in the bathtub, she was right in front of him so he tried to help her. To begin with, he couldn't touch her, his hand kept going through her,'

'That's right…'

'But then, just before she vanished, he got *wet*… the water from the bath soaked him, it was real… he touched it.'

Jack didn't know what to say to that, had no explanation for how it could be possible. 'OK… So that's… weird, I'll give you that.'

'So they *can* touch us, they are real.'

'I don't know. We'll find out, though, like I said. That's what we do.'

'But the fat man…'

'Don't worry about him,'

'You don't understand… If he can touch us, he can *hurt* us…'

Jack suddenly noticed a curious smell.

Julia was pointing over his shoulder.

'He's behind you!' she shouted.

The fist, a sweaty, pink baseball bat of fingers, hit Jack in the small of his back, making him cry out with pain. His leg gave way beneath him as the two fat hands clasped his head, the wet palms oozing over his face, the smell of sweat and sex so strong on them that he felt the urge to gag.

'Run,' he said to Julia through mashed lips, though she hadn't waited to be told, pulling herself out of the room and to the top of the stairs where she began shouting for help. Her words were muted, Jack's ears sealed shut beneath the man's grip, but he could see the force of them in her red cheeks and the spittle that flew from her lips.

He grabbed his attacker's wrists – refusing to even think about the impossibility of such a thing; like he'd said to Julia, answers always came in the end – forcing his thumbs into the tendons, trying to stop the crushing grip and the probing of nails dressed with brown crescents of dirt into his eyes and mouth.

There were bright white explosions in his eyes as the pressure increased. He stamped down with his feet, desperately trying to kick his attacker, shatter a knee, perhaps, or break a toe. Fat he may have been, but he was strong too. He shook Jack and squeezed hard, stealing the force from his blows.

Jack was quite convinced the man was going to kill him. While this wasn't the irrevocable catastrophe for him that it was for most people, he had little doubt that the man wouldn't stop at one victim. Having promised Julia he would keep her safe, this bit deep into his conscience. Why hadn't she just run? He saw her move into the main bedroom… What was she doing? He wasn't to find out – his attacker shoved him towards the floor, and there was an awful cracking noise in his ears as the man's foot came down on the back of his skull.

# FIFTEEN

It had been a matter of some determination on Alexander's part not to worry about anyone else in life. It wasn't just that he was a misanthropic old git – though that was certainly the case – it was that being, quite literally, an illegal alien in the arse-end of one of the more unattractive and unenlightened galaxies was hard enough without bringing the sensibilities of others into it. Put simply: he had enough on his plate. Which is why it irritated him that he couldn't stop wondering what Jack was up to. He had been hired to poke Torchwood's stiffs (and positively crisp in the case of Gloria Banks) and the rest of their business was most certainly none of his.

Still, the situation was rather intriguing. Albeit, he had concluded, not in the biological sense. The two humans had died through rather self-evident causes: one had choked and one had burned. The interest lay in how either of those things was possible. It was infuriating to be teased by these unusual circumstances and yet play no deductive part in them. He was Mrs Hudson to Captain Jack's Holmes. How despicable. Alexander couldn't abide the thought of being a bit part in anyone's drama.

He would join in their investigation, and to hell with their opinions on the matter. He spun his wheelchair around and looked up the flight of metal stairs.

Just as soon as he figured out a way of leaving the building.

Rob heard the sound of Julia screaming and was determined to run to her aid. If only he could move.

What was happening to him? He was struggling to recognise himself any more. The reflection in the kitchen window was the portrait of someone he knew, a decent man he was sure, a kind and gentle man, one who loved his wife and would never do anything to harm her. Someone not at all like him. How he wished he could make the pressure in his head go away. All he needed was peace and quiet. A little time on his own.

Of course, it would help if that silly bitch upstairs could just stop screaming.

He heard the woman – Gwen had they called her? – run upstairs. Taking the opportunity to move while nobody would notice him, he slipped out of the kitchen, opened the under-stairs cupboard and climbed inside.

He sat down on a box of old newspapers and sniffed

the reassuring odour of old ink and dusty wood, the scent of carpet and damp and age. It was a quiet smell, a relaxing smell. He shoved his fingers into his ears and tried to ignore the thumping of feet above him, the frantic toing and froing of those determined to break his calm.

Julia was terrified and yet determined to stand up for herself. The last couple of days had seen her lose a sense of strength that she had spent most of her life trying to build. Bit by bit it had been chipped away until she was close to being struck insensible by her fears. It had to stop.

She stared at the fat man over Jack's shoulder, taking in the details of him for the first time. His features fought for space in the middle of his face: piggy eyes, button nose, puckered mouth, all surrounded by a sweating pink tyre of skin. The sweat soaked into his suit, dark brush strokes that painted out the brown pinstripes. He rippled in his taut clothing, reaching out with arms that seemed as wide and meaty as carcasses lifted from abattoir hooks. He'd punched Jack in the back before grabbing his head like a ball he planned to throw a very long way.

'Run,' Jack had said, and she had, shouting to the others downstairs and then running through to the main bedroom where Rob had left his toolkit. She grabbed the best weapon she could find, a long-barrelled screwdriver, and – reminding herself over and over again that if a man was solid enough to hurt others he was solid enough to *be* hurt – ran back to the spare bedroom.

She found his solidity strangely reassuring; he had been far more unnerving to her when she had believed him insubstantial.

He threw Jack to the floor and Julia barked her anger as she saw him stamp on the back of his head. Someone was running up the stairs behind her, but she was determined to stake a claim on this moment, to snatch back a little of that strength before it was beaten out of her completely.

She thrust the screwdriver at the bloated face, unable to maintain her grip as the tip dived into the cave of his mouth and his teeth grazed her knuckles. It seemed he wished to eat the screwdriver as he had done so much else.

He vanished, just like the woman in the bath – spluttered a few bubbles of blood onto her outstretched hand and then was gone.

'Julia?' Gwen burst through the doorway behind her.

'I'm all right,' Julia replied, trying to hold on to that fragile wave of confidence she had just felt, the sight of Jack's head robbing her of it as she looked at his flattened, damp hair. 'But he's…'

Jack's body suddenly thrashed, and he rolled over with a yell of pain.

'Please tell me he didn't give me a bald patch!' he shouted.

Julia gave a shriek of surprise and fell backwards, Jack rushing to grab hold of her.

'I'm sorry,' he said. 'Remember what I said about magic?' She nodded. 'Good, because I'm the smooth-talking, cool-walking living embodiment of Clarke's third law!' He grinned and gave her peck on the cheek. 'Now what say we get on with getting those cameras rigged?'

It was at the highest point of the winch, suspended some four or five metres above the Autopsy Room, the hoist chain wrapped around the arms and legs of his wheelchair, that Alexander began to wonder whether this hadn't been a rather stupid idea.

Rob, listening to the banging and crashing upstairs, reached for the catch on the under-stairs door in a moment of confusion. Shouldn't he be out there helping? Making sure Julia was all right? Then the pain in his head began to return, a pulsing in his temples as if something was rupturing just to the side of his eye. He stuck his hand out for support, gripping the shaft of the taped-up croquet mallet and squeezing it as hard as he could, as if that would somehow transfer the pain from his head to the wood.

The momentum of Alexander's swing over the gantry railing was enough to drag the length of chain out of the winch and leave it trailing behind him like an enthusiastic millipede. If it hadn't been for his collision with some metal shelving, his injuries could have been much worse. He swore as he toppled forwards, following the shelves and the junk on them, leaving his wheelchair far behind.

'Stupid bloody Torchwood,' he muttered, wincing as he felt something cut into him where he had landed on it. Pulling what appeared to be a crab made of iron ore out of his side, he flung it at the pteranodon in case that insistent cawing it made was laughter. 'Shut up or I'll extinct you,' he threatened, pulling himself back into his chair and making for the one of the desks. Now… where had they gone?

Julia needed Rob. Captain Jack's gleeful lack of concern for the laws of physics was all very well – and reassuring in its own way – but she wanted her husband alongside her. She hadn't seen him for a while; he'd stormed off in a sulk while Jack had been sorting out the cabling in the dining room, and Julia had been inclined to leave him to it, given his mood. Enough now, though. Where was he?

She was scrubbing the back of her hand with a nail brush. Although there was no sign of any blood on the inflamed skin, she was finding it hard to imagine it could ever be clean.

'Don't go to the loo from now on without drawing the shower curtain,' said Jack behind her. He was standing in the bath, a small camera fixed to the tiles behind him. 'It'll cover up the lens.'

Julia nodded and carried on rubbing at her hand.

'That's enough now,' Jack said, stepping out of the bath, taking her hand and rubbing it gently between his own. 'The blood's gone.'

Julia felt tears in her eyes, and she bit her lip. She was

determined not to give in to that any more. 'It might be commonplace to you,' she muttered, 'but I don't normally go around shoving tools in people's mouths.'

There was an awkward pause at that and then, despite herself, she burst into hysterics. 'I'm sorry,' she said. 'That came out so wrong… I wasn't having a pop about you being, you know…'

'He prefers the term "omnisexual",' said Ianto, stepping into the room. 'It's the polite way of saying he'll sleep with anything – men, women… cephalopods. I must be the only boyfriend that's ever had to get jealous in a fishmongers.'

'Don't knock the sensual embrace of the tentacle,' Jack replied with a wink.

'Oh God…' Ianto replied. 'I could have died happy had I never heard you say that. Changing the subject – cos one of us has to before someone throws up – I've disconnected four monitors, the amp and a couple of speakers, so we're all set.'

'Isn't he wonderful?' Jack said to Julia, kissing Ianto on the forehead. 'What would I do without him?'

'The same things you do with me, just to someone else,' Ianto deadpanned.

They walked out of the bathroom and into one of the empty rooms on the top floor.

'OK…' said Jack. 'So who forgot to tie the rooms down?'

# SIXTEEN

Joe was starting to lose his rag but trying not to show it.

'I'm on my way, babe,' he promised into his mobile, 'but the gig ran late, and we had to fight for our money.' There was an earful of panic and Joe rolled his eyes. 'No... not really fighting... It's just an expression, isn't it?' He swapped ears and blew some of the rain off his nose, moving as quickly as he could across Roald Dahl Plass without slipping. That'd top the night off, flat on his back with a smashed guitar and Martinette dumping him for always being late. 'I'm getting the car now... Yes, straight there... Promise... Love you too, babe, and I'll see you in— Oh.'

There was an old man lying on the ground, a wheelchair on its side next to him.

'Some old bloke's had an accident,' Joe told Martinette.

'Fallen out of his wheelchair or something… No, of course I'm not making it up!'

He ran over to the man and turned him over. 'Bloody hell,' he whispered. 'I hope he's not…'

'Freezing his ageing knackers off waiting for some sap to walk over and help?' Alexander moaned. 'Yes, I'm rather afraid he is.'

He sprayed the contents of what looked like an inhaler into Joe's face, grabbing the mobile out of his hand before he dropped it. 'He'll call you later,' he said into the phone, cutting it off before the shouting on the other end got into full flow.

'Now,' he said, yanking the battery out of the back of the phone to disable it, 'that surprisingly potent drug that's running through your system is a little something I knocked up myself. There shouldn't be any long-lasting effects – none that your girlfriend will complain about anyway – but you'll find that for the next few hours you'll be inclined to do whatever anyone tells you.' He pushed himself up on his elbows. 'So how about getting me back in my wheelchair and giving me a lift to Penylan?'

'Why not?' said Joe with a doped grin that made it look like he had bad wind.

'Some kind of spatial displacement?' asked Ianto.

Julia groaned, 'I'm not up for much more of this.'

'If this is like what happened to me,' Ianto said, 'vanishing from one place and appearing in another, how come we're not all a bunch of ice cubes?'

'It's a question of energy,' Jack replied. 'The worse this situation gets, the less juice it takes to move a body from one place to another. Heat is the most readily available energy source in a human being. It took most of yours in the jump from outside to here. Now… well, things are becoming really disturbed, so moving between locations in space-time is becoming dangerously simple.'

He grabbed Julia and Ianto's hands. 'It's OK, though, we'll be safe enough. Let's just…'

They walked out of the room and reappeared in the kitchen.

'Hmm. Let's just try and get back to where we want to be.'

He kept talking as they walked through the kitchen door…

'This kind of disturbance can't last long.'

… into the lounge. Out of the lounge…

'Or if it does, the damage to the physical cohesion of this part of the universe will be so immense…'

… onto the upstairs landing.

'… we'll be beyond caring.'

They ran down the stairs, walked through the door to the dining room and were relieved to find themselves in it.

Gwen looked up from unknotting cable and stared at the three of them.

'Sweet,' she said, noticing that they were all holding hands. 'Glad you're all getting on so well.'

\*\*\*

'It's bloody freezing in here,' moaned Alexander, twisting and wrenching at the heating controls.

'Heater doesn't work,' chuckled Joe.

Alexander glanced at him. He had the feeling he'd miscalculated the dose – the young man seemed positively euphoric. 'You live in Wales,' he said. 'You need a heater in your car, you silly masochist.'

'You try earning your living playing the guitar in pubs,' Joe replied. 'See how many luxuries you can afford.' He started to laugh uncontrollably.

Alexander sighed, reaching out to steady the wheel as Joe's giggles made him swerve. 'Get us there in one piece, and I'll buy you a new car.'

'Cool!'

Joe put his foot down and began singing as they motored their way through the one-way system.

'I need to find Rob,' Julia insisted. 'Has nobody seen him?'

'Not for a while,' Gwen admitted, 'but I'm sure he's OK.'

'In this place?' asked Julia, looking towards the dining room door. 'Do you think it's safe?'

'As much as it'll ever be,' Jack replied. 'Ianto, would you…?'

'Of course.' Ianto put his hand on Julia's arm. 'Let's go and find him.'

Jack started wiring the loose video and microphone cables to the equipment on the dining room table.

'I hope Rob's OK,' said Gwen. 'Things are getting pretty serious here.'

'So what's new?' Jack replied. 'Rob's bound to be freaked out, but he was handling it better than a lot of people would.'

'The first time we met him, he tried to bash your head in with a poker,' Gwen pointed out, 'and we're in a building that excels at sending people mad.'

'There is that,' Jack admitted as he began tuning the monitors in to the video feeds.

She turned her laptop screen towards him, the scan of an old newspaper on it, 'Recognise the face?'

Jack glanced at the screen and stopped what he was doing. The grainy black-and-white image showed an exceedingly large man being led away from the front door of Jackson Leaves by two police constables.

'I didn't see him,' he admitted. 'He attacked me from behind. Seems likely he's our man, though, doesn't it?'

Gwen nodded. 'Rupert Locke, convicted of six violent rapes in 1951.'

Jack shrugged. 'Don't remember him.'

'I'm surprised. There looks to have been a lot of coverage about it. He was completely unrepentant. Told the police "the house made me do it".'

Jack banged his hand against the table in frustration. 'That's the problem with all of this,' he said. 'It would have set alarm bells ringing at the time if I'd read it. It's hardly subtle, is it?'

'How do you mean?'

'All of these things happening around Jackson Leaves – a house I owned – you think I wouldn't have looked into it before now?'

'Perhaps you were too busy to notice? Being in Torchwood, it's easy to miss some of the more... conventional stuff.'

'I might have missed some of the news reports, sure, but *all* of them? No... there's something skewed about this. If it had been going on all these years, I would have known about it already. OK, so Torchwood wouldn't have looked into it, the incidents are all typical police business and they would have had no reason to spot the link, but I would. I'd have had *every* reason.'

Ianto and Julia came back in.

'He's not here!' Julia said. 'How is that possible? We've checked every room, and there's no sign of him.'

Jack finished plugging in the video cables and turned on the bank of monitors. Each showed an empty room of the house. Flicking through the feeds it was plain that the only inhabited room was the one they were standing in.

'He might have gone outside,' Gwen suggested.

'Of course he hasn't!' Julia spat. 'Not after what we saw.'

'There's only one explanation, then,' said Jack. 'He must have vanished through one of the rents in space-time.'

'What?' Julia was incredulous.

'We've got repeated bursts of temporal and spatial distortion,' Jack explained. 'Something is causing space to fluctuate – like when we left one room and found ourselves in another. Ianto "fell" into one of those fluctuations and ended up here. Rob must have done the same, ending up—'

'Who knows where…' Julia bit her lip. '*Anything* could have happened to him.'

'I hate to say it,' Jack offered, 'but if he's out of this place he's probably a lot safer than the rest of us.'

'Think how Ianto was,' Gwen added. 'I'm not saying it was pleasant—'

'It certainly wasn't,' Ianto agreed.

'— but you were OK in the end,' Gwen continued, giving him a slightly admonishing look.

'Damn right.' Jack put his hands on Julia's shoulders. 'If he's got out of here, then he'll be fine, just like Ianto was.'

'I don't know…' Julia looked at Jack, her body shaking. It was all finally getting on top of her.

'Do you trust me?' he asked.

Her eyes glanced around, her panic building, barely in check. 'I don't know…'

'You *need* to trust me, Julia. I've seen us all right so far, haven't I?'

She nodded. 'I suppose…'

'Yes, I have, and I'll get us all out of here safely…'

'And Rob…'

'And we'll find Rob, and everything will be just fine. Now listen, I need you to take this.' He handed her a pill and a half-full bottle of mineral water.

'What…'

'I need you to trust me, Julia, it's important. I wouldn't hurt you, now would I? Take this, and then we'll find Rob.'

She stared at him for a moment, then her shoulders sagged and she gave in, tossing the pill to the back of her throat and washing it down with the water.

'What are you giving her?' Gwen asked.

'Retcon, of course,' Jack replied.

'Oh Jack,' Gwen sighed. 'You didn't have to do that.'

'What?' Julia asked. Her head was tingling, like pins and needles behind her eyes.

'Sorry,' Jack said, 'but it's for the best.'

The penny dropped and Julia tried to run, but the drug was quicker than she was. She stumbled in the hallway, falling against the under-stairs cupboard as her legs refused to support her.

Gwen chased after her, holding up her arms to defend herself from Julia's weak blows. Slowly, the woman crumpled, the fight gone from her. Gwen looked up at Jack.

'You can be a pretty heartless bastard sometimes, Jack, you know that?'

'I just have a sense of priority,' he replied. 'We need to fix this, and she was going to be in the way. She'll be fine.'

'She'd better be.'

Jack rolled his eyes in exasperation. 'We have to see the bigger picture here, Gwen! Have you no idea how much trouble we're in? Right now, she is the least important problem we have – it's nothing personal, it's just fact – and I used the quickest and safest way of removing that problem.' He looked at Ianto. 'Right?'

Ianto ignored him, helping Gwen to pick up Julia's body. 'We'll put her in the lounge,' he said. 'She'll be comfortable there.'

Jack sighed. There were times when he wondered if they'd abolished pragmatism in this century.

Beneath the stairs, Rob was barely even aware of what was going on outside any more. The noise of his wife falling against the door to his private little world didn't even register as he hugged the taped-up shaft of the croquet mallet, digging his teeth into the wood and listening to it whisper awesome potentials into his head.

Some of the things it suggested in the dry creak of its wooden tongue were terrible, but he knew he would do them. And when they finally stopped him, put cuffs on his wrists and led him away, he'd tell them the truth knowing they wouldn't believe a word of it.

'The house *made* me do it,' he'd say.

# SEVENTEEN

'Right,' Alexander said, checking the coordinates on the PDA he had stolen from a desk in the Hub against the street map. 'It's that house over there.'

He pointed at Jackson Leaves, just visible over its unruly privet hedge.

'Brilliant!' Joe shouted. 'Does that mean I can start singing again?'

'No it bloody doesn't,' Alexander replied. 'One more "Sweet Home Alabama" out of you, and I'll make you eat the steering wheel.'

'Oh.'

Alexander swore and whacked the edge of the PDA against the dashboard. 'Stupid thing's on the fritz, can't seem to make its mind up where we are. Let's get out and have a look.'

'Great!' Joe grinned and started swaying as if he was in a nightclub.

'I am definitely checking the dosage,' Alexander sighed.

'Do you want me to get your wheelchair?'

'No, I'm cured, it's a pissing miracle.'

'Wow!'

'Of course I want my wheelchair!' Alexander shouted.

Joe chuckled and got out of the car. By the time he'd got the boot open he was singing again.

'Right,' said Jack, as Gwen and Ianto came back into the dining room, 'we need to talk.' He kept flicking his way through the camera feeds, checking each room. 'You both think I'm heavy-handed. But the more I think about what's going on here, the more I think I need to be. How is she?'

'Sleeping on the sofa,' said Gwen. 'She's fine.'

Jack flicked a switch, and the lounge appeared on one of the four monitors. Julia was hunched, foetal, on the sofa.

Jack nodded. 'Good.'

He stretched in his chair, his lower back still hurting from where Locke had punched him. A purple and yellow bruise would certainly be blossoming there by now. 'This isn't investigation any more,' he continued, pointing at the monitors. 'This is surveillance. We need to know the minute something tries to get a jump on us. I'm starting to piece this together, and it's freaking me out.'

'I was there from the word go, frankly,' Ianto said.

'Something is causing major time disruption,' Jack continued. 'Think of the deaths: Danny Wilkinson drowns on dry land. But it wasn't always – go back a few centuries and that was marshland out there. You saw a woman killed by a tram that stopped running along that street years ago. Gloria Banks… I don't know, she sits down in her armchair and…'

'Bursts into flames,' Gwen finished.

'Yes! It could have been anything. Perhaps a bonfire was there once… or, I don't know, maybe it was a blacksmith's at some point?'

Gwen had been tapping on her laptop and she turned it around to show them. 'Or, during the Blitz, a bomb went off a few hundred metres away and the house was caught in the blaze.'

Jack glanced at the council report she had brought up. 'Exactly.'

'Blacksmith's?' asked Ianto with a smile.

'Whatever.' Jack rolled his eyes. 'The point is that something is causing temporal disruption on a massive scale. We're not just seeing things; these aren't after-echoes.' He turned to Gwen, thinking of their conversation earlier. 'This isn't residual haunting. The past has *weight*, it can interact with us, drown us, burn us…'

'Stamp on our heads,' Ianto added.

'Yes! Rupert Locke… he's certainly not floating around is he? When he appears, he's actually *here*. It's as if the two time periods are folding over one another, layered with each other, physically co-existing for a brief period. When the walls were pounding, maybe that was just the Jackson Leaves of fifty years ago trying to co-exist with the Jackson Leaves of today, the two slightly out of place over the years because of subsidence.'

'Subsidence?' Ianto smiled at Gwen. 'Or maybe just the spatial disruption?'

'Yes.' Jack nodded. 'Maybe. Because it isn't just time, is it? Something is distorting physical space.' He glanced back to the monitors, flicking through and making sure all was clear before turning back to them. 'I can't put into words how that scares me,' he said. 'You just don't start messing with existence like that. It's pretty elastic, but if you screw with it for long enough it'll snap.'

There was a flash of movement on one of the screens.

'Did you see that?' Ianto shouted.

Jack and Gwen turned to the monitors.

'It was one of the top rooms,' Ianto said. 'A woman…' He stared at the screens, infuriated at the lack of anything in them. 'I know I saw her… She moved across the room towards the door. A woman in a long white dress, maybe a wedding gown.'

Jack felt his heart trip. 'You sure?'

'Yes! A woman in a long white dress, she moved across the room towards the door.'

They kept scrolling through the camera feeds.

'She's not there now,' Gwen said.

Jack got to his feet.

'Where are you going?' Ianto asked. 'There's not much

point in setting all this up if you're just going to leg it up there and have a look for yourself!'

Jack closed the door behind him and began running up the stairs.

Joe was wheeling Alexander along the pavement towards Jackson Leaves, Alexander keeping himself dry under an umbrella he'd found in the boot of the car. He didn't offer to share it, but Joe didn't care. He was singing 'My Generation' at the top of his voice and was quite happy, thank you very much.

'Shut up,' Alexander ordered. Joe did. Alexander sighed and waited to have to tell him again; each command seemed to afford him about two minutes of silence. 'Stop here,' he said, a few metres from the house. He stared at the building and tried to decide what it was that disturbed him about it.

'There's something not right about that house,' he said, thinking aloud.

Joe looked at the building for a few moments before giving up and going to dance in the street.

Alexander studied it for a while then wheeled himself to Gloria's front garden, where he selected a lapful of small stones. He returned to Jackson Leaves, parked a little way back from the drive and began to throw the stones.

'Oh no!' Joe giggled. 'You can't do that, we'll get in trouble.'

'Just watch me.' The stones flew towards the house but vanished long before they got anywhere near it.

'Hmm,' Alexander said. 'What does that tell us, Joe?'

Joe stopped dancing for a moment. 'Time for a pint?'

'No. Unless there's some form of force-field technology screening the building – and there isn't because you can always tell, force fields give off static like it's going out of fashion, makes your hair follicles go tighter than a fly's arse – it tells us that Jackson Leaves isn't altogether *there*. Which is rather strange.'

'Yeah!'

'Wheel us next door, Joey my lad,' Alexander said, pointing to the house the opposite side to Gloria's. 'We need some equipment and a dry place to work.'

'OK.' Joe pushed him along the pavement. 'How are we going to convince whoever lives there to help?'

'My dear Joe, I could have you pushing this wheelchair along with your tongue if I wished, couldn't I?'

'Yeah!'

'Good. Then you just leave the convincing to me, all right?'

Alexander chuckled. He could get used to field work, he was really rather enjoying himself.


Hadn't Jack cautioned himself about getting caught up in his memories? Here was the result, chasing through the focal point of a space-time collapse with a head full of guilt and no clear plan of action. To think earlier he'd been preaching pragmatism.

'Follow me on the camera feeds,' he shouted.

\*\*\*

In the dining room, Ianto jumped forward to turn the volume down as Jack's voice came through loud enough to make the speakers shake.

'Oh, righty-ho, then,' he muttered sarcastically, shaking his head at Jack's comment. 'We'd never have thought of that.'

'What do you think set him off?' Gwen asked, ploughing through the Jackson Leaves documents on her laptop, hunting for any mention of a bride.

'You heard me say there was a woman on the screen, did you?'

'Now, now,' Gwen admonished playfully.

Jack reached the top floor, both rooms were empty.

'Nothing,' he said.

'I could have told him that from here,' said Ianto, 'though that would have cut down on his "looking dramatic" quota for this evening.'

'You're getting more sarcastic with each passing day,' Gwen said.

'It's the only pleasure I have left.'

Gwen raised an eyebrow, but didn't comment. 'Nothing here obviously relating to a woman in white,' she tapped her laptop screen, 'but then it wasn't a huge deal to go on, was it?'

Ianto leaned forward in his seat. 'I'd say she was about my height with long black hair. From the look of her dress, I'd place her at the earlier part of the twentieth century or maybe late nineteenth.' He pointed at the screen where the woman had appeared in the room Jack wasn't. She moved towards the door and promptly vanished.

'Jack?' Ianto stabbed at the audio buttons. 'Oh, come on… patch in your earpiece…' With a roar of exasperation, he got up and opened the door to shout up the stairs.

'Hello!' said Rob, standing in the doorway holding the croquet mallet. 'Sorry, but the house made me do this.'

He swung the mallet.

# EIGHTEEN

'Hello, my dear,' said Alexander as the girl opened the door. 'My name is Alexander Martin, and you would be furthering the safety of the universe were you to let my friend and me use your facilities.'

The girl, about sixteen or seventeen, leaned out of the doorway and scratched at her mop of curly hair.

'Your friend would be the tit getting jiggy in the shrubbery, would he?'

Alexander swallowed with embarrassment. 'That's him.'

'Piss off.'

She was closing the door as Alexander hit her full in the face with the spray he'd used on Joe. 'Dear lord,' he sighed. 'I'm not sure I can stand both of you acting like mental outpatients, but I suppose I have little choice.

What's your name, my dear?'

'Hannah Ogilvy.'

'Splendid. Well, Miss Ogilvy, are you by any chance alone in the house this evening?'

'Yeah.'

Alexander visibly slumped with relief. 'Right then. Joe!'

'Yes, boss?' Joe appeared behind his chair waving at Hannah like a five-year-old who's just been introduced to a big purple dinosaur.

Alexander looked at him for a moment and then wheeled himself into the house. 'Never mind, Joe, change of plan. Stay out here.'

'Cool!' Joe spun off into the rain, dancing and singing.

Rob suddenly felt a moment of clarity. He had been sitting very still, occasionally chewing on the head of the croquet mallet but otherwise not moving. Then it was as if something had turned on in his head. He knew it was time to step outside the cupboard and get on with the suggestions the house had put to him.

He heard the heavy boots of the American pound up the stairs above his head. Once they had passed, he reached out in the dark and opened the catch of the door, stepping into the hallway and stretching his arms, letting the muscles pop back into place after being hunched for so long.

The prissy one in the suit – the one they should have shoved back in their airing cupboard and forgotten all about – was shouting on the other side of the door. Rob grinned at the humour of it all. He loved a bit of slapstick, a bit of rough and tumble. As the door opened, he showed his happy teeth to the invader of his house. 'Hello!' he said. 'Sorry, but the house made me do this.'

He swung the mallet, but the man got his arm up in time to stop it doing any major damage. Rob was sad. It just wasn't so funny if the punchline wasn't the sound of the young man's forehead splitting open. The invader threw his weight against the door, shoving it closed. Rob roared with anger.

'Stop spoiling the joke!' he screamed. 'Stop spoiling the joke!' He hammered against the door with the mallet, sweat flicking off his vein-lined forehead with exertion until he stopped abruptly, reached into his pocket, pulled out a key and locked the door. 'Ha Ha,' he said in a flat voice. 'Two keys.' He leaned close to the wood. 'I'm going to do something bad now. Bye.'

On the third floor, Jack's body was fizzing in response to the air around him. When you had travelled in time enough to begin developing a somewhat loose attitude towards the here and now, you became sensitive to changes in the temporal fabric around you, as if the skin itself were more aware of the flow of seconds and minutes. It felt the same as when a television was left turned on in a room, its screen blank – that charge in the air, the flow of particles across the glass that radiated out and made the hair on the back of your neck stand up.

As Jack walked towards the corner of the room, he became aware of the charge increasing in the air around him. Suddenly the room changed and he found himself looking on it in better times, the wallpaper and paintwork crisp and new, no cobwebs or dust. He stopped moving and tried to feel the static in the air, holding out his hands and tickling the chronons with his fingertips. Sensing a surge to his left, he aimed for it and found himself back in the present day.

He moved onto the landing, the tingling getting stronger all the time. Things were close to falling apart, time and space becoming no more than a jumble around him. By the stairs, he felt a wave of chronons and, sticking out his arm, watched the hand disappear as it left this point of space-time and entered somewhere else. Leaning forward, he stuck his head through where he estimated the hole to be. He found himself looking down on Rob and Julia as they slept in the main bedroom, Rob snoring while Julia – eyes slowly widening in fear – looked up at Jack's face and recognised it for what it was.

Jack pulled himself back onto the landing and moved into the other room.

'Jesus!' Ianto shouted as he came face to face with Rob in the doorway. Gwen jumped up from her seat, the sound of panic in Ianto's voice more than enough to get her moving. Ianto got his arm up in time to stop Rob doing any damage, darting back and shoving the door closed while Rob was unbalanced.

'Tell Julia I've found her husband,' said Ianto, pressing hard against the door to keep it closed as Rob pounded on it from the other side.

'Stop spoiling the joke! Stop spoiling the joke!' Rob screamed.

Gwen was looking around for something to use as a weapon, even as they heard the lock click and Rob's whispered threat.

'Oh no…' she said, flicking the monitor switch and watching as Rob walked away from the door and towards the lounge where his wife lay sleeping. 'We need to get that door open before he harms her!'

'Right!' shouted Alexander, surrounded by a mess of cannibalised electronics. 'Now we might be getting somewhere.'

Hannah was silent, staring at the abandoned shell of the microwave, the television and her mobile phone. In contrast with Joe's euphoria, the drug seemed to have made her maudlin, and Alexander was quite perplexed by it. Human beings did have such remarkably chaotic biology.

'Now then,' he said, looking forlornly at her, 'do try and look interested. I hate not having an audience when I do something clever. What we have here,' he held up the ugly combination of his PDA and the household items he'd scavenged, 'is not unlike the gadget that young Ianto had for tracking chronon signatures…' He stopped himself, realising the pointlessness of what he was doing.

'You have no idea who I'm talking about. Doesn't matter. With any luck, it will help me find a point of access to that very strange house next door.'

Hannah sighed and kicked a piece of the microwave across the floor. 'Whatever,' she said.

'I think, on reflection, I prefer the dancing buffoon outside,' Alexander said, dumping the apparatus in his lap and heading back towards the front door.

Jack was in the middle of the street. To his left was the half-built shell of a house, to his right there was little but rubble and open earth. Looking directly ahead, he saw the open foundations that would soon become Jackson Leaves, moonlight falling on cement sacks and timber, piles of brick and grit.

'You'll grow up to be trouble,' Jack said, stepping backwards and reappearing by the window in the upstairs room.

There was the sound of frantic hammering from downstairs, and he dashed towards the door, jerking to a halt as the air around him suddenly changed, thickening, coalescing into liquid. His legs came out from under him and he fell backwards. Looking up, floating in the murky water that had overlaid itself on the structure of the room, he found himself staring into Alison's terrified eyes, her hair flailing around her screaming face as hands pressed down from above. Jack reached for her, desperate to help, and his hands brushed on another's fingertips, but something had him by the ankles and he began to sink.

Looking down, he could make out the shape of the river weeds swaying in what little moonlight made it this far beneath the surface of the water. If he could just untangle his feet... He looked up as he tugged at the weeds, watching Alison's panicked movements begin to slow, arms cutting through the water more and more dreamily before the scream on her face sagged into an open-mouthed expression of absence. It seemed to him that he saw the life fade from her eyes. They went from shining green glass to dull as earth. Miles's hands let go and vanished into the air, even as what was left of Alison headed towards Jack, seemingly for an embrace. As she sank, so did he, dropping onto the threadbare carpet of the third-floor room, his clothes as heavy from the river water as his heart was with guilt.

Neither Gwen nor Ianto saw Jack as he disappeared then reappeared in the room above. They were far too occupied in trying to force the lock on the dining room door, fighting not to be distracted by the sight of Rob entering the lounge on the monitor screen beside them.

Rob stood by the arm of the sofa, cradling the mallet in his arms as one would an infant. He looked down at his wife, stroked her forehead with the back of his hand and smiled as she began to come round. Her eyes were glazed with the drug in her system, and when she looked up at him it was first with confusion then with a rather sleepy smile.

'There you are,' she said dreamily.

'You can see me?' he asked.

'Yes,' she said, though her eyelids were drooping.

'I wish I could,' he said, his eyes dampening. 'I was beginning to think I was completely lost.'

Julia was falling asleep.

'Please don't,' Rob said, touching her face again.

'Hello?' she said. 'Tired…'

'Yes,' Rob nodded. 'They poisoned you.' He rubbed away the beginnings of tears. 'We're both poisoned.'

'He talked about drugging us,' Julia murmured. 'Remember? Threatened it… to make us do what he wanted.'

'All poison makes you do what it wants,' Rob replied. 'This house is the same.'

'Need sleep.'

'I know you do… I hope the drug does make you do whatever someone says. If it does… well, that makes this easier.'

'What do you mean?' asked Julia.

'I love you, Julia, OK? Forgive me for what I'm about to do.'

Julia smiled. 'I do.'

Rob sobbed and raised the mallet above his head before bringing it down with all his strength.

As Jack sat up, a stone broke through the glass of the window, bouncing off the wall and rolling into the corner of the room. He didn't notice, getting to his feet in a daze and stepping onto the landing. There were three doors now, rather than two. He stared at the new door, fixed in what could only be an external wall.

Another stone burst through the window next door.

Jack reached out to the brass knob of the impossible door, opened it and stepped out of Jackson Leaves altogether.

# NINETEEN

As Jack stepped through the door, a bell rang above his head, its chime mixed with the sharp hiss of a milk steamer, but it wasn't quite loud enough to drown out the sound of Gene Vincent on the radio. He closed the door behind him, and looked out through the dirty glass that had replaced the wood. Outside was the slow, weekday drudgery of work traffic, lorries and vans, moving things from one place to another.

'Morning, my lovely,' said the woman behind the counter. 'What will it be?'

Jack walked carefully between the tables. A group of spotty-looking mods eyed him from the corner. One of them, working hard at looking more than his meagre years, peered from behind the turned-up collar of his Fred Perry shirt and started tapping his fingers on the formica in an attempt to intimidate. It did nothing of the sort; as a man who had once helped Keith Moon get a Cadillac into a hotel swimming pool, Jack would need a little more sign of the young man's credentials before he felt even vaguely daunted.

The woman behind the counter wore her dark roots with the same confidence as the stains on her waitressing uniform. Stitched into her faded Gingham breast was the word 'Durdles', though whether that was her name or the café's he couldn't guess. She looked at him through glasses whose bright red rims brought no cheer to her tired eyes.

'Well?' she asked again, patience as thin as her happy veneer.

'Coffee,' Jack said. 'Sweet and milky.'

'I'm not your mother. Sugar's on the counter.'

So it was, though the spoon was chained down in case he had the hots for their cutlery.

She wrestled with the machine as if it was going out of its way not to produce. It roared and hissed like feral cats in a slowed-down piece of film, vapour ejecting from the pipes with the industrial vigour of a power station. She vanquished it eventually, wringing a mug of frothy coffee from out of its guts.

'Thanks,' Jack replied, cracking the crust on the sugar bowl and spooning in a couple of shards.

'You're welcome to join me,' said a woman's voice behind him.

He walked over to her table and wedged himself as

comfortably into the orange plastic seat as physics would allow.

'This is all very real,' he said, puffing gently on the white coffee froth to cool it.

'Reality is so subjective, wouldn't you say?'

She was an elderly woman, hair an immaculate grey confection as rigid as a plastic hat. She wore wool in layers: a pullover, a cardigan and a skirt that crackled when she moved, as soft as a scouring pad. Jack recognised her from the reports Gwen had shown him.

'Is there a particular reason why you look like Joan Bosher?' he asked.

'Not really, though we were rather impressed with her – such a strong sense of self, she never snapped, never lost control. Not many of your species could say the same.'

'We're a fiery lot, it's true.'

He took a sip of his coffee. It tasted of wet air, but he couldn't decide if that was proof of this fantasy's strength or weakness, British coffee in the 1960s had been pretty lousy.

'So, you wanted to see me?' he asked.

'We were curious,' she admitted.

'You're not the only one.'

'Oh, we're not so interesting,' she said, brushing imaginary crumbs from the table top.

'Like reality, interest can be subjective.'

She smiled, and for a moment the room seemed to bend with her lips, the walls rising and the tables distorting as the floor formed an upward arc that followed the curve of her good humour. Then her mouth straightened and the room with it, the floor flattening out with a loud bang.

'True,' she said, as if the contortions around her had proved her point. 'We are from …' she inclined her head as if checking for the words, 'a potential dimension. Somewhere outside what you know of reality…' She smiled again, though this time the café had the decency to stay still. 'But then so much is. Your view of existence *is* rather limited.'

'That's humans for you, terribly parochial.'

'We will make considerations. You are only very basic life forms after all.'

'Too kind.'

'Not at all. As a species, we have a… I think you would call it *hunger*… for temporal damage.'

'You feed off paradoxes?'

She looked up at the ceiling, and Jack tried not to notice the delicate ripples in the pale, wrinkled flesh of her throat. He didn't know whether it was due to a failure in concentration or a deliberate attempt to freak him out, but there was certainly more than blood moving in her veins.

'That's as close to correct as we will manage, I think,' she said finally. 'Forgive me, but it is complicated, like you trying to explain maths to a dog.'

'I'll work hard to keep up.'

The mods in the corner laughed, though whether at him or not he couldn't tell.

A shadow fell across the room as something unseen

flew past the front of the building. Nobody paid it any attention.

'We find a point of interest,' she continued, 'somewhere that already has a delicious flaw, a *potential*.'

'The Rift,' Jack muttered.

'Oh no!' she laughed, the vibrations of her mirth shaking all the tables in the café. 'We barely noticed that until after we'd latched on to your universe. It was *you*! You light up this continuum like a beacon.'

The shadow passed again, this time flipping across the backs of the vehicles as the unknowable creature that cast it landed on the roof.

'The damage you have done to the time stream is almost incalculable,' she continued. 'Come from the future, steal from the past… I lost count of how many of you we detected in – using your relative year markers – 1941.' She reached out and took his hand. 'You get so involved! The first rule of time travel, my dear, leave the locals alone – if you don't want to attract our attention –' she smiled and her teeth stretched like clarinet reeds from her gums, long, yellow and eager to cut and chew – 'and believe me you *don't*. Changing things, people and events, that draws attention. You're a force of nature, Jack, a temporal tsunami, and we *tasted* you.'

Her tongue fell between the elongated rows of teeth, flopping onto the back of his hand where it curled and licked, enjoying the salt of his skin.

He tried to pull his hand back from her grasp, but she held it tight.

'We found that little house of yours, where, as always, you did so much damage…'

'What damage?'

'So unrepentant! My darling boy, there were two time lines damaged before you'd even had time to let the welcome mat gather dust.'

Jack became aware that there was a couple sitting at the table next to them. He knew it was Miles and Alison without even having to turn. Could tell by the cool drips of river water he heard fall from Alison's slack mouth onto the formica.

'Small fry by your standards, I'll admit,' she continued, dabbing the tip of her tongue on the web of skin between his fingers, 'but the building had such potential. So, we reached for it…' she extended a bony index finger, 'and *pushed*…' her fingertip disturbed the air around it, sending out ripples, 'forcing ourselves further and further into the universe.'

'Why didn't I notice?' Jack asked, tilting his head as the ripples from the disturbance in the air ricocheted off his brow.

'We've only just started, barely longer than this conversation in your relative time. Our presence echoes all the way along the building's time line, altering things, distorting them… But your position as a time traveller offers you something of a unique perspective. You remember the past the way it was *before* we started to interfere. Jackson Leaves wasn't always the soup of violence and paradox that it is now; we just *made* it that way – in less time than the waitress took on your drink, mark you. All the better to feast when we reach inside far enough.'

She bit at the knuckle on his little finger, drawing a drop of blood, before letting go of his hand and withdrawing her tongue back inside a shrinking mouth. Within moments she was just simple Joan Bosher again.

'And we will feast soon,' she added. 'You've time to drink your coffee but not much more than that.' She pushed the mug towards him.

Jack got to his feet and walked towards the door. He yanked it open and swore as he found the road on the other side. Above his head he could hear the sound of whatever dream creature perched on the roof as it tightened the grip of its talons on the guttering. He stepped back into the café.

'Just drink your coffee,' said the thing that looked like Joan Bosher. 'Once feeding has been instigated, there's no turning back.'

'Relax,' suggested the waitress, picking up her dirty cloth and dragging its mouldy fabric over the counter. 'It's only a universe, after all.'

'Take the weight off,' said the more aggressive of the mods, walking towards him.

'Just lie back…' added Miles, looking toward his waterlogged wife.

'…and take it,' Alison gurgled.

Jack thought for a moment before marching over to the mod, picking him up by the lapels of his parka and hurling him through the glass of the door. The glass shattered and the mod winked out of existence, even as the room in Jackson Leaves reappeared on the other side of the fracture.

'Don't lay the table just yet,' warned Jack, stepping through the hole in the door and back into his universe.

# TWENTY

Alexander's wheels cut channels through the rain as he headed back towards the front of Jackson Leaves, the umbrella wedged behind his shoulder to keep both him and the apparatus dry. If anything, the rain seemed to be getting heavier, bouncing off the road in white sparkles, and flooding the drains, running in great streams along the gutter. Alexander noticed the streetlights begin to flicker as he lined himself up with the drive of Jackson Leaves.

'It's getting worse,' he whispered, his words lost in the clatter of the rain.

Joe and Hannah didn't need him to tell them, though; looking around was clue enough. The privet hedge writhed in front of the house, new growths shooting forth, leaves unfurling into dry then dead, knocked apart by the hammering rain. A season's growth in an instant.

'It's spreading out,' Alexander shouted, pointing at Gloria Banks's house next door. The structure seemed almost fluid, windows fluctuating between shattered holes and bright new glazing, giving the impression that the house was winking at them. Maybe it was pleased at the undulations that were taking place across its surface: cladding surging forth to be sucked back in again by the hungry bricks, clouds of cement dust exploded from the grouting as it moistened then aged. The blue-granite gravel that Gloria had taken such pride in was not serving her well, swirling and spluttering as it was whipped to and fro by the weeds that thrashed within it.

A crack appeared in the pavement just in front of Alexander's wheelchair.

'We need to be quick!' he shouted. 'Joe, fetch a couple of stones – not from there!' Joe had been moving towards Gloria's house. 'Idiot! Behind us. The disruption is less the further one goes from the house.'

Alexander turned on the contraption in his lap and pointed it towards Jackson Leaves. On the PDA screen he could see the swirls and eddies of chronons as the disruption fluctuated over the area.

Joe returned, holding out a pair of stones.

'Right,' said Alexander. 'Let's test this, shall we?'

He took the stones, weighing them gently in his palm as he scrutinised the PDA screen.

'Listen, the two of you,' he shouted. 'With this, I can see the disruption waveforms. They ebb and flow, yes?

Like a tide… rippling towards us. If we're quick and precise, I should be able to guide our way, picking the point at which the waveforms are stretched thin and less dangerous… like… there!'

He threw the stone and, instead of disappearing as it had before, his good aim saw it sail through the disruption and break the glass of one of the upstairs windows.

'Aha! What did I tell you?' He threw the other stone and it followed the trajectory of the first, rewarding the three of them with the sound of more glass shattering. 'There *is* a route through the waveforms, see?'

He looked at them, but what he was saying was so far beyond their understanding of physics it clearly meant nothing. 'Look… just imagine we're on a beach facing the sea, OK? We want to get into the deep water but can't let the crests of the waves touch us as we go in. If they touch us we will die, so we have to *jump* them. You understand?'

'Like the seaside!' Joe shouted.

'I hate the bloody seaside,' moaned Hannah. 'You always get sand in your…'

'Yes!' Alexander roared. 'Just like the seaside. Now, Joe, you'll have to carry me on your back, the wheelchair will just slow us down.'

'Piggyback ride!' chuckled Joe, dropping down in front of Alexander's wheelchair. Alexander passed the waveform reader to Joe and clambered onto his back, holding the umbrella over both of them to keep the equipment dry.

'Hold the screen right out in front of us,' ordered Alexander, 'but remember it's not waterproof, so keep it under the brolly, yes?'

'Yep!' Joe stood up and gave Alexander a playful bounce. 'This is going to be fun.'

'I sincerely doubt that,' Alexander replied, staring carefully into the screen. 'OK, so we need to take two steps to our right…'

Joe did.

'And then forward four steps on my mark, one… wait for it… two – stick close, Hannah – three… now!'

'I hope the drug does make you do whatever someone says,' said Rob's voice on the speaker. 'If it does… well, that makes this easier.'

'No!' Gwen shouted, knowing only too well what he was about to do. She began kicking violently at the door, her hip and ankle flaring in pain with each blow.

'What do you mean?' asked Julia on the monitor, while Ianto yanked out the drawers in the old dresser, hunting desperately for anything he might use to force the lock.

'I love you, Julia, OK?' Rob promised, as, drawer after drawer, Ianto came up with nothing. 'Forgive me for what I'm about to do.'

Gwen swore. There was no way she could break through – the wood was too thick and she was working against the frame. She couldn't give up though. One last try…

Julia smiled. 'I do.'

Gwen ran at the door, roaring at the top of her voice. Just before she hit it, she vanished, space folding in on itself from the pressure of dimensional intrusion.

In the lounge, Rob sobbed and raised the mallet above his head before bringing it down with all his strength…

Gwen, appearing from the wall by the fireplace, barrelled into him, her momentum sending both of them to the floor.

Rob was quick to recover. He kicked out at Gwen, reaching for the mallet which had gone flying in the scuffle. His foot caught her on the hip, which was sore already from her attempts to break down the door, but she clenched her teeth against the pain and fought to stay close. The last thing she wanted was to give him the space to use his weapon.

Rob grabbed the taped shaft of the mallet, but reaching out had left him open to attack. Gwen utilised every ounce of combat training, following the cardinal rule of punch-ups: there's no such thing as a fair fight. She thumped him hard in the groin and, while he was curling into a ball, got one hand on the mallet. Her other hand found the back of his head, grinding his face into the carpet.

She pushed herself to her feet, yanking the mallet out of his hands and was about to hit him with it when a hand dropped onto her shoulder.

'Don't,' said Jack. 'It's not his fault.'

'OK,' said Alexander. They were now standing on the

gravel forecourt of Jackson Leaves. 'That didn't kill us, then. How wonderful.'

'Time to build sandcastles?' asked Joe.

'Maybe later, my boy,' Alexander replied. 'Let's see if any of Jack's lot want to come out to play first, eh?'

Jack unlocked the dining room door to find Ianto standing there with his arms folded.

'When you've all finished being heroic in my absence,' he said, 'I'd quite like to have a go myself.'

'You can start by figuring a way out of the house, then,' said Jack.

'Oh,' Ianto wandered into the hall. 'That hardly seems fair… All Gwen had to do was beat up a workman.'

There was a knock on the door. Ianto turned to look at Gwen and Jack.

'Don't ask me,' said Jack.

Ianto opened the door, and a young man barged past him with Alexander on his back.

'Hello there,' the old man smiled. 'Did someone order a genius?'

# TWENTY-ONE

'It's not his fault,' someone said, and Rob Wallace had to agree.

Opening his eyes, he was surprised to find himself back in his and Julia's old flat, cluttered but familiar, the place they had always lived together. Perhaps he had dreamed Jackson Leaves? It certainly felt like it. Pounding walls and ghostly visions… not the sort of thing that happened in a real house. Houses were normally pretty reliable places: bricks and mortar, mortgages and electricity bills.

He was thirsty. Stepping into the little open-plan kitchen, he ran his fingers over the jumble of magnets and notes on the fridge door. These were the things of proper houses, he thought, reassuring and colourful, postcards from Spanish beaches, shopping lists filled with loaves of bread and bottles of milk. Julia had bought one of those random 'build-a-poem' magnet sets, a jumble of words that you shuffled around to make new verse. He read her last effort: 'Wander out into the sky / Ask your self the reason why / Clouds that love are full to burst / Open mouth and feel their thirst.' Rob smiled. It wasn't exactly Pam Ayres, but at least it rhymed. He pushed the words 'your' and 'self' closer together, trying to fix her grammar, but the gap remained obvious. He supposed it should be allowed.

He closed his eyes and shuffled the words around with his fingers, lining some up to form a random sentence. He opened his eyes and read what he had made: 'Burst your love feel the sky and thirst.' Very poetic. He closed his eyes again and started dragging other words in from the cool white page of the fridge door: 'Show her no tears / From a man who know / His fears are real / His death will show.' A lucky rhyme, but it was getting rather morbid…

He closed his eyes and shuffled them again. 'Show her a man who love death and tears / Burst the sky and know real fears.' No… he didn't like that game any more. The words kept making him feel as if there was a message in them, something he didn't want to know.

He opened the fridge, and looked for something cool to drink. There was a bottle of fizzy water, Julia's favourite. To him it tasted like pop with the fun taken out, but he was thirsty enough to drink anything, unscrewing the cap and drinking straight from the bottle. There was a bad smell in the fridge, something rotting. He had a poke around but couldn't find anything obviously mouldy, just a lot of different meats, damp and pink, perfectly fresh.

He closed the door and found himself feeling terribly lost in the middle of the kitchen. A ridiculous feeling in such a small space, but at that point he felt smaller. Felt, in fact, as small as one could be, stranded on the cheap black-and-white floor tiles as appliances towered over him – the jagged kettle, the sheer, silver austerity of the toaster, the towering black glass of the oven. He found his breath catch in his chest and reached for the radio, desperate to break the atmosphere with noise. He was momentarily certain that the cooking knives would eviscerate him for such a move, chop away his naughty fingers into little pink rings, but they stayed happily embedded in their wooden block, and the radio hissed into life as he turned the dial.

'Tie him up with that,' said an American voice.

'Tightly,' a woman added.

There was the screeching sound of heavy-duty tape being yanked from the roll.

Some sort of drama, perhaps? Or an advert? He wasn't sure what the sounds of a man being bound would entice him to buy. He tried changing the channel, but there was nothing else but static so he turned it back. He would have preferred music, but this was better than nothing.

'Julia's out of it,' the woman was saying. 'Someone will have to carry her.'

*Where* is *Julia?* Rob wondered, reminded of his wife by the characters in this strange programme – she always complained that Julia was such a common name, you heard it everywhere. He'd gone online to look up the name's origin; it was the feminine form of 'Julius' which meant 'man with downy beard'. He'd pulled her leg about that for weeks.

'OK!' the American on the radio shouted. 'Thanks to Alexander, we have a way out and all of you need to take it, *now*.'

'Oh, shut up, you big bully.' Rob muttered, turning off the radio.

The silence was still uncomfortable, so he made his way out of the kitchen and across their little lounge to the television. There had to be something cheerful and breezy on, something to take the edge off his stupid nerves. At first he could find nothing but static, ghost images, half-shapes and jagged lines. Then, flipping through the channels, he found a picture: people all sat in a roadside café, an old woman talking to a soldier – at least Rob assumed he was a soldier, he was wearing an old uniform, certainly, though clearly he wasn't on duty as his collar was open. At the table next to them, a woman was dripping water all over the table and floor. Ridiculous. Perhaps it was supposed to be a comedy?

The camera moved to a close-up of the old woman, and Rob banged the side of the television, trying to improve the reception. The poor signal made it look like there were things crawling under her skin.

'That's it, Rob,' the old woman said, making him dart back from the screen. '*Hit* me.'

Rob stabbed at the remote control with his index finger, desperate to flush the woman from the screen.

'No,' she whispered. 'Not like that… like this!'

She swung her arm, and Rob felt the sting on his cheek as if he had been struck.

'How did you—?'

She hit him again, his cheek glowing hot with it.

The radio suddenly crackled back to life.

'He's completely out of it,' said the voice of the woman he had heard before in the advert about tape.

'I'm not…' he said. 'At least, I don't think I am…'

'You could have fooled us,' said the old woman on his television. 'Dead from the neck up… Isn't that what you are?'

He felt his cheeks turn cold and a pressure building in his sinuses.

'What are you…?' He ran to the bathroom, wanting to see his face in the mirror. It had lost its colour, turned the pale blue-grey of necrotic tissue. He rubbed it with his hands, and it felt thick and damp, like a verruca.

'Is that better?' the old woman asked from the next room. 'Is that what you like?'

Rob wanted to cry but knew that his dead tear ducts had no liquid to shed. He scratched at his cheek – wanting to feel something – and his nails filled with dead skin. He could just feel the touch of his fingers; perhaps his real face was still there, hidden underneath this useless hide? He began to peel, cautiously at first but then – as he realised it didn't hurt – in the biggest chunks he could get hold of. The sink filled with it, like cool, undercooked chicken meat, and soon there was nothing left for him to look at in the mirror but bone. There was no point in continuing to dig. There was nothing left of him.

He was lost.

'Rob?' Julia's voice, coming from the bedroom. 'Where are you, Rob?'

He made his way through to the poky room that was just wide enough to hold the double bed they had made their own. Julia lay on the rumpled duvet in her wedding dress. The gown had certainly known a happier day; now it was falling apart, shedding flakes of taffeta and lace like the peelings of sunburned skin.

'Is that you?' she asked, staring straight up at the ceiling.

'Yes… it's me,' Rob replied, touching the wet bone of his jaw and realising he must be beyond recognition. 'My face… something happened to it.'

'Something always does, doesn't it, Rob?' she chuckled. 'There's always one problem or another, one mistake you'll never make again… Until you do, of course, over and over and over… I don't know why I bother with you.'

'Please…' Rob was confused. Why was she being like this? 'Don't say that. I try so hard… I really want to make everything great… And I will, you wait and see, we'll make a real go of it in the new house…'

And suddenly he was uncertain again, did they even have a new house or was that the one he'd dreamed up?

He hated to show his confusion but hated not knowing more.

'We do have a new house, don't we?' he asked her.

She made a scoffing noise in her throat. 'Not any more, you saw to that. So weak…'

'I am not!' Rob scared himself with the ferocity of his shout; he hadn't known it was coming. He had to be careful of his anger, that was something he did remember. It was too strong sometimes.

'You see,' said the voice of the old woman from the television next door, 'that's your problem, always reining in your strength. That's why you lost the house, because you gave in.'

No. Rob began to shiver. He wasn't to let his anger loose. Anger wasn't strength, anger was…

'Turning yourself in circles,' Julia laughed, 'tying yourself in knots, so pathetic… How I hate you…'

'Don't…' Rob felt the anger building.

'… hate you, hate you, hate you, hate you…'

'Please…' Rob's fingers were clenching, his jaw locking, muscles popping as they strained to be flexed.

'… hate you, hate you, hate you, hate you…'

'Pathetic man,' added the woman from the television. 'What are you *for*?'

'Shut up!' Rob shouted.

And woke up…

# TWENTY-TWO

'I barely touched him,' said Gwen, as Ianto rolled Rob over and they both stared into his vacant eyes.

'You don't know your own strength,' Ianto replied. 'What should we do with him?'

'Tie him up with that,' said Jack, handing him a roll of gaffer tape.

'Tightly,' Gwen added.

Ianto tore a length off the roll and started wrapping it around Rob's wrists. Gwen moved over to the sofa. 'Julia's out of it. Someone will have to carry her.'

'Great,' Ianto sighed. 'Half of us need carrying out of here.'

'Or dragging,' Gwen muttered, eyeing Rob.

'You'll manage.' Jack smiled and stepped out into the hallway.

'OK!' he barked so everyone could hear him. 'Thanks to Alexander, we have a way out and all of you need to take it, *now*.'

'And what do *you* propose to do then, oh loud, shouty one?' asked Alexander, who was sitting on the stairs to give Joe's shoulders a rest.

'This house is the locus for something forcing its way into our universe,' Jack replied. 'Unless we do something about *that*, there's no point running *anywhere* – everything will cease to exist in the next few minutes anyway.'

'You have a plan, of course?' asked Ianto from the lounge doorway.

'Naturally,' Jack grinned. 'If the house is the door, then the easiest thing to do to stop anyone getting in is… get rid of the house!'

Ianto stared at him for a moment and then nodded. 'Good. Fine. Great plan. Good luck with that, then.'

'I know what I'm doing, but I don't have time to discuss it. Trust me,' Jack replied, cupping Ianto's face and kissing him on the cheek.

'Wahey!' shouted Joe.

'Do excuse the boy,' said Alexander. 'He's enthusiastic to the point of agony.'

'I know the type,' Ianto replied, stepping back into the lounge. He stared down at Rob. 'I know you can walk,' he said. 'Nobody slips into a coma because they have their balls punched.'

'I have powers,' said Gwen.

'A way with testicles, certainly.'

Gwen dropped to her haunches by Rob and slapped him hard on the cheek. After a moment she did it again.

'He's completely out of it,' she said, walking out into the hall.

'Thank you, Nurse Cooper,' Ianto muttered, trying to wrestle Rob onto his shoulders.

Jack worked his way through the storage compartments in the rear of the SUV, grabbing a couple of packs of plastic explosive and a timed detonator, then walked back into the house.

'Definitely a subtle plan, then?' Alexander joked, spotting the explosive.

Gwen came out of the lounge.

'I need to borrow your friend,' she said to Alexander. 'Julia's a dead weight, and he seems a strapping lad.' She grinned at Joe, who, of course, grinned back.

'Strapping,' he said.

'Very well,' Alexander sighed. 'Hannah? Your turn on piggyback duty.'

'Oh God!' Hannah moaned, walking over to the stairs. 'That is *so* unfair.'

'I'll have you know that there are many civilisations who would consider it an honour. Besides, look at me – you've worn heavier coats in your time.'

She mumbled under her breath but had no choice but to let him climb on.

'Who are these two, anyway?' Jack asked.

'Deputies,' Alexander replied. 'I drafted them to the

cause. You owe Joe a new car and Hannah some kitchen equipment.'

Jack shook his head. 'Whatever. We can worry about them later.' He turned to Gwen. 'Keep your eye on them.'

She nodded. 'Of course.'

'OK… Now will you all get out of here?' Jack began herding them through the door.

Ianto and Joe grunted their way out of the lounge, only one of them smiling. As soon as everyone was outside, Jack slammed the door behind them, took a deep breath and ran up the stairs.


'Hold it still!' Alexander moaned, trying to track the waveform movements on the PDA screen as Hannah held it up for him.

'Whatever,' she whinged, though the drug in her system was still in full effect so she froze like a statue.

Alexander gripped the brolly tight against the force of the rain and compared the readings in front of him to the driveway ahead. It was getting much harder to tell, the ripples moving even faster now as the disruption increased.

'I think…' he said, screwing up his eyes and trying to find the weak points, 'I think it's over…'

'Shut up!' Rob roared, thrashing on Ianto's shoulders and sending both of them tumbling to the ground. Rob was quick to his feet, grabbing the PDA from Hannah's hands and pushing Alexander from her shoulders.

Alexander shouted in pain as he landed badly, the sound of his wrist snapping audible even over Rob's ranting.

'Get out of my house!' he was screaming. 'Give me back my wife and get out!'

'Did nobody think to bind his legs?' Alexander shouted.

'What do I do?' Joe asked.

'Oh, give her to him!' Alexander replied. 'Just get the waveform reader back or we'll never get out of here.'

'No!' Gwen shouted. 'Keep her away from him, Joe.'

Joe made a childlike whining noise. The drug programmed him to obey, but it didn't care who was giving the orders. He didn't know what to do.

'Typical,' Alexander moaned, cradling his broken wrist. 'We're about to get caught in a time-space collapse, and Torchwood Girl wants to worry about an abusive relationship. Let the apes do their thing, I say.'

Rob was moving perilously close to the edge of the drive and the waveform. 'Burst the sky and know real fears!' he shouted, fragments of his dream returning to him.

Ianto had rolled over to the SUV. Reaching into the glove compartment, he pulled out the spare handgun he knew Jack made a habit of stashing there.

'Hand the reader over,' he shouted, pointing the gun at Rob, 'and… well… stop being such a pain in the arse, frankly.'

'Oh, very good,' Alexander muttered. 'But I think

we can all see he's beyond the point of negotiation.' He beckoned Hannah closer and began to whisper in her ear.

As Jack moved up the stairs, he could feel the air shifting around him. The entities must be close to entering, reality was beginning to fall apart. At the first-floor landing, Kerry Robinson held out her opened wrists to him, dripping more than bath water onto the carpet at her feet.

'It'll stop hurting soon,' he promised her as he ran past and up the next flight of stairs.

He wasn't surprised to see Alison floating high in the corner of the upstairs room, but was careful to avoid stepping too close. He didn't have time to get caught in the reeds of her little bubble of hell.

'I'll do what I can,' he said, moving carefully across the floorboards, trying to find the doorways he'd experienced before. He only hoped they were still…

He found himself in Rob and Julia's bedroom, both of them now thankfully asleep. Carefully, he backed up into the upstairs room and worked his way around the tear in space-time, waving his fingers in front of him to find its edges.

If that one was still there then that meant… his hand vanished up to the wrist in front of him.

He was briefly aware of the smell of onions before he stepped forward and vanished.

***

'Life's so unfair,' moaned Hannah, walking towards Joe.

'Stay back!' Rob shouted. 'I just want all of you out of here, go on…'

'Idiot,' Hannah said to Joe. 'Give him the woman, as long as he hands over the thing in his hands, and ignore what anyone else says.'

'Oh…' The relief on Joe's face was immense. 'Hey, mister, do swaps?'

Gwen tried to push Joe back, but Hannah punched her in the jaw.

'That hurt my bloody hand!' she shouted, walking alongside Joe towards Rob.

'There,' Rob said, throwing the PDA to Hannah. 'Now hand her over.'

Hannah put the PDA on the floor and ran at Rob screaming and crying simultaneously. 'Life's so unfair!' she screeched, jumping at Rob and knocking both of them back into the waveform.

They were caught, twisting slowly as the ripples of space-time distortion pushed and pulled them, ageing bone and peeling skin, hair growing only to become dust.

'Stay back!' Alexander shouted as Ianto ran forward to try and help. 'There's nothing to be done.'

The two of them became less distinct as they broke up into chunks, pebbles, grit, then dust, dissipating around the waveform like sugar stirred into coffee.

'You made her do that!' Gwen shouted at Alexander.

'Oh shut up and grow a pair,' Alexander muttered. 'I

did what had to be done. Now pass me the reader and hope the rain's not completely…'

‘He's gone!' Joe wailed, ‘What am I supposed to do with her if he's gone?' He whirled around in distress and stamped on the PDA.

# TWENTY-THREE

Jack stepped out into a Penylan night at the turn of the twentieth century. Taking a breath of fresh air to cleanse his palate after the oppressive, static-filled atmosphere of Jackson Leaves, he walked to the centre of the hard concrete foundations and began to set his explosive charge.

'I can't see how you think that would help,' said a voice to his right.

He looked up and, squinting in the moonlight, tried to recognise the speaker. 'Alison?' he asked, then shook his head. 'No, of course not.'

'I thought you might prefer her to old Joan.'

The creature walked over to him and squatted by his side as he pushed the timed detonator into the plastic explosive.

'Is it that you just like destroying things?' she asked, lying back on the concrete. The illusion was perfect, the cool, evening breeze erupting gooseflesh all over her body as she squirmed in the dust.

'He can't help it,' said another voice from behind him and he wasn't altogether surprised to see Miles – or a perfect copy of him at least – walking towards him. 'He's a man, and we just love to break things apart.'

'Oh,' said Alison. 'I always thought better of him than that.'

She licked her lips and, even in the low light, Jack could tell the tongue was far too long, rolling across her cheek before dipping its tip into the corner of her eyes to drink.

'No you didn't,' he replied. 'At least the *real* Alison didn't – she knew me much better. She was under no illusion that I was anything but trouble.'

'How right she was,' said the Miles creature. 'I wonder if that's what she was thinking as I drowned her.'

Jack shook his head and placed the explosive on the ground. 'I imagine she was wishing she had agreed to marry someone much more stable.' He began to walk away. 'I didn't kill her. That arrogant, image-obsessed and deluded lover we shared did.' He turned back to them, trying not to notice how much their fake humanity was slipping as their bodies twisted in the darkness. 'I can't take the blame for everything that happens to people I know. Miles killed her because he couldn't stand who he was. That's sad but it's hardly my fault.'

The creatures gurgled deep in their throats, a sign of anger, Jack presumed. Miles, on all fours, began to scuttle back and forth, while Alison stretched along the floor, her biceps and thighs stretching like toffee as she writhed, limbs snaking away in different directions.

'You are ceasing to be an entertainment,' she said, her voice taking on a hollow quality as it bounced around her elongated chest. 'You would do well to stop this now before you anger us further.'

'Or what?' Jack asked. 'You may be close enough to this universe to make yourselves seen, but if you're that powerful, tell you what, stop the bomb yourself. Go on, all it takes is a finger on a button.' He smiled. 'You can't, can you? You have no real physical presence here, you're just voices and cheap threats. A pair of ghosts.'

Miles reared up, pulling at his dream skin as if even the pretence of flesh was a discomfort to him. 'What do we need hands for,' he asked, the words distorting as he yanked at his mouth, pulling his cheeks out into a loose trumpet, 'when we have puppets to do our work for us?'

Jack smelled Locke before he felt him, but not soon enough to avoid the blow that sent him to the floor in a spiral of cement dust.


'You stupid idiot!' Alexander roared at Joe. 'I've a good mind to send you running into the waveform.'

'You try it, and I swear you'll follow him,' Gwen warned.

Ianto tucked the handgun into the back of his trousers.

'You thought you knew where the safe passage was,' he said to Alexander.

'What are you talking about?' the old man snapped.

'Just before Rob woke up,' Ianto reminded him. 'You were looking at the reader screen and you thought you knew which way we should go.'

Alexander tried to remember. 'Yes…' he said. 'It was about there…' He pointed to the far left of the drive opening. 'But that hardly helps – it's not just about location, it's *timing*. We would have to move just as the waveform was at its weakest point.'

'Like ripples on water?' Ianto asked. 'When the waves are at their furthest reach, the centre is at its calmest.'

'Yes, and we can't possibly tell when that is without using the waveform reader.'

Ianto climbed into the SUV and began to perform a three-point turn.

'Careful!' Alexander shouted as the wheels nearly ran over him. He looked at Gwen. 'What does the boy think he's doing now?'

'I don't know,' Gwen admitted.

Ianto positioned the car so that it was facing the privet hedge, set the headlamps on full beam and got out. Pulling the gun out of his waistband, he turned towards Jackson Leaves. The house was beginning to lose cohesion now, windows running like mercury into the melted wax of the brick. He aimed the gun at the outside light and fired. The bulb shifted slightly in the distortion and the shot missed. He fired again, this time allowing for the movement and the bulb shattered, leaving the headlights as the only illumination.

'When you've quite finished taking pot shots at the bloody house,' Alexander said, 'perhaps we might like to come up with a plan for getting out of here.'

'Look at the rain,' Gwen said as Ianto walked over to Alexander and picked him up off the ground.

Shining in the beam of the SUV lights, the pattern of the rain as it followed the contours of the waveform was clear, glistening ripples sweeping across the pitch-black absence of the outside world beyond the limits of the house.

'Careful!' Alexander whined, his broken wrist twisting against Ianto's body as he was hoisted up. He stared at the water pattern as Ianto walked right up to the edge of the driveway. 'You know, lad,' he chuckled, 'you might just have cracked this… Now, careful, it's all a question of…'

Ianto threw him at the barrier, where he vanished into the darkness.

'Timing?' he said. 'Looks like it works to me.' He turned to Gwen and Joe, who was still carrying the unconscious Julia over his shoulder. 'Who's next then?'

Locke used his size to great effect, dropping onto Jack and knocking the wind out of him. Jack screwed his eyes against the bad halitosis and a slow dripping of blood that fell from Locke's mouth like a damaged tap. Behind them, the facsimiles of Alison and Miles scampered to and fro, whipped into excitement by the violence.

Locke made to grab Jack's face, hoping to grind it into the concrete, but Jack aimed a strong punch at the big man's armpit and sucked grateful air as Locke squealed and rolled off him. There was no doubt who had the advantage as long as he was on top, but Jack was fitter and back on his feet quickly, while Locke was still cradling his dead arm.

'I'm sorry,' Jack said. 'For all I know, you were a nice enough guy before they got to you.'

'Him?' Alison said. 'He was an accident waiting to happen, a dirty little primate.'

Jack picked up a spade that had been left by the workmen.

'There's nothing wrong with dirty primates,' he shouted, bringing the flat of the spade down on Locke's knee and grimacing as he heard it break. 'I happen to be one of them.'

He dropped the spade, disgusted by the violence, but only too aware that the stakes were too high for him to treat anyone gently.

The timer on the explosive continued to tick down. Two minutes left…

'It won't stop us!' Miles shouted. 'So you cause a little damage… They'll just rebuild, fill it in and start again.'

'Of course,' said Jack as he began to walk away. 'But it'll delay things for a bit, and that's all it needs to shift the time line. I certainly won't end up buying the place. It caught me on a whim. As long as I don't buy it, you won't have used it as your locus, and… guess what?'

'What?' Alison asked, slithering towards him.

'You told me that once your feeding cycle had started it couldn't be stopped. That right?'

'Yes…' Miles hissed.

'Well, the minute the new time line snaps into place, you do know what the biggest paradox will be here, don't you?'

The creatures looked at one another.

Jack smiled. 'That's right! *You. Bon appétit.*'

The creatures continued to shift, losing all sense of humanity, before leaping on one another with a roar.

Jack turned and walked back towards where he had appeared, holding out his hands to feel for the gap in space-time he had come through. The tips of his fingers tingled as they found the fluctuation in the air, and he stepped through into an upstairs room in Jackson Leaves.

The house wouldn't keep still as time ebbed and flowed around it. The walls kept changing, wallpaper and paint flowing and vanishing as every moment in its history played out, fighting to find a constant. History had been altered around the building and now he had altered it again – a ridiculously dangerous thing to do, but the only option he'd had open to him.

Now time was trying to find a steady path, acting out every conceivable permutation. The house was built in 1906, then it wasn't. He bought it, then he didn't. As he walked out of the room and into the hall, it was like trying to fight his way through a piece of speeded-up film in

which he was the only constant. Alison – the real Alison
– was there, running naked down the stairs chased by the
ever-hungry appetite of her strange lover.

Miles appeared as Jack reached the next landing. Even
at a glance, Jack could tell he was pleased to see him…

'If only you could have been as happy in your body as
I was,' Jack whispered, holding out his hand to stroke the
ethereal chest of one of the many men he had once loved.
His fingers jolted as if he had brushed an electric fence,
and the image of Miles vanished.

Jack kept walking, fighting the urge to look into the
other rooms. He could hear other lives playing out in
them, couples fighting and making up, children laughing,
as they ran from one room to another before vanishing
altogether, perhaps never to have existed there at all.

He stood for a moment on the landing, as he felt
the most bizarre sensation wash over him. Just over a
hundred years ago, he had stood at this very same spot,
showing Alison the house. The words he had spoken
bubbled up from him, but when they reached his ears he
knew it was his past self that was speaking them.

'Do you like the house?' he had asked, leaning over the
banister.

'It could be lovely,' Alison replied, as she moved up
towards him, 'with a woman's touch.'

The ghost of Jack, smiled down at her. 'I say again: just
like its owner, then.'

'Anyone's touch will suffice for him,' came Alison's
reply.

'But your touch is the sweetest.'

The present-day Jack found himself cringing at the way such easy lies and promises fell from him time and time again.

Alison stepped onto the landing, and he had to remember that she was not looking at him but rather the man he had been all those years ago. 'So you say today,' she said, 'but who will it be tomorrow?'

Ah… and didn't he know the answer to that from his vantage point in the future?

His past self took Alison in his arms. 'Stay the night and find out.'

Jack reached out to them, spreading his arms to cover them both, ignoring the sting of temporal flux that clung to the lovers' shoulders. The ghost of Alison shivered.

'You all right?' asked the Jack from her time.

She nodded. 'It felt like something touched me.'

Jack let go and stepped back. They were not his to hold any more.

'Give me a few moments and it certainly will,' his past self replied.

'Really…' Alison said. 'Perhaps you've got ghosts…'

He certainly did. Moving past the translucent figures, Jack ran down the stairs, knowing that by the time he reached the bottom they would have vanished for ever.

The fluctuation was near breaking point by the time he got to the front door, the roar of the hundreds of residents who had lived – or might have lived – between these walls becoming deafening in his ears. He grabbed

223

the door handle, wrenched it open and stepped out into…

… daylight and shouting.

The SUV was still parked at the front of the house (though it was now pointing out towards the road), and Alexander was lying on the pavement cradling his broken wrist.

'How dare you!' he roared at Ianto, who was standing over him. 'Do you know who I am, boy? I will not be treated like that by *anybody*, let alone a jumped-up little shit like you.'

'Shut up,' Gwen muttered, wheeling the old man's wheelchair over from where she had found it further up the road. 'You should be glad you're alive. Not everyone is, thanks to you.'

'Problem?' asked Jack as he joined them on the pavement.

Ianto grabbed him and gave him a stifling hug. 'Not that I was worried or anything,' he muttered self-consciously as he let him go. 'Plan worked, then?'

'Guess so.'

Jack turned and stared up at Jackson Leaves. It looked the same and yet… not. It was tidier, more looked after, no longer the abandoned relic it had once been. 'What happened?'

'We made it out,' Alexander hissed, pulling himself into his chair and gritting his teeth against the pain in his wrist. 'No thanks to your lot, I might add.'

'He killed the girl,' said Gwen, suddenly feeling even worse as she realised she didn't even know her name.

'I dealt with that lunatic you saddled us with,' Alexander replied. 'The girl was caught in the crossfire. If I hadn't acted, I doubt any of us would still be here. If you got down from your high horse for a moment, you would do well to realise you should be thanking me rather than wailing about a little collateral damage.'

'Thanking you?' Gwen said. 'If I had my way, we'd be locking you up.'

Alexander smiled, and it was one of the most unpleasant things Gwen had seen all night. 'You just try it, girl. I've dealt with worse than you've got to offer.'

'Shut up, Alexander,' said Jack, 'before I do what Gwen suggests. Let's just look after these two.' He pointed at the still unconscious Julia and Joe, whose exuberant mood had well and truly faded, leaving him confused and hung over, leaning against one of the lamp posts.

'By all means,' Alexander replied, unable not to have the last word in the matter. 'Just so long as you remember you would do well to keep me sweet. I could be a considerable irritant to you otherwise.'

'You mean you're not already?' Ianto lifted Julia into the back seat of the SUV as Gwen took Joe's arm and led him over.

Jack looked down at Alexander. 'Don't do it,' he whispered.

'What, my dear boy?' Alexander replied, that oh-so-false smile still in place.

'Bite off more than you can chew.'

Alexander shrugged. 'I don't *want* to make enemies.' He gave Jack a look that was altogether more powerful than one would expect from such a frail-looking man. 'So don't force me to.'

Jack shook his head dismissively, and they headed over to the vehicle.

They dropped Alexander back at the rest home.

'What about my wrist?' the old man whined as Jack pushed him towards the building.

'Physician, heal thyself,' Jack replied, leaving him at the front door and dashing back to the car.

'You're just going to leave him?' Gwen asked as he got back in. 'Knowing what he does?'

'His biology is so far removed from ours, I wouldn't have the first idea what to do about it,' Jack admitted as he turned on the ignition and drove away.

'Well, I don't trust him,' Gwen said.

'Me neither, but he'll have to be a problem for another day. We've enough to deal with for now.'

'At least the house is safe,' Ianto piped up from the back.

'No more ghosts,' Gwen added with a half-smile.

'Oh, I don't know about that,' said Jack and drove back to the Hub.

# TWENTY-FOUR

TORCHWOOD CARDIFF: INCIDENT REPORT

Unexplained Conflagration
Penylan, 17th March 1906

Visited the site of last night's explosion,
found residue of non-contemporaneous
explosive material and signs of temporal
flux. (Gaskell's Chronometer Device threw a
fit, solely, it seems, by virtue of being
in the same street as the bomb damage!)
Bizarrely, the target seemed to be nothing
more than a building site, nothing of
imaginable value. Harkness proved little help
- one had hoped his knowledge of futuristic

methods might have helped to shine the light
of clarity on some of the more outré elements
of the incident, but he pleaded ignorance so
well that one might be inclined to believe
him, were it not for the fact that he lies
with such ease. No matter; no civilians
were hurt and, while the evident intrusion
of foreign agents in our jurisdiction is
alarming, there is some consolation to be
found in that. Our investigation will, of
course, continue.

AG

Ianto smiled and dropped the sheet back into its folder. Alice Guppy's writing about Jack always reminded him of a strict teacher's report on an errant student.

He glanced over at his workstation, where his screen was a blizzard of files and news reports, history rewriting itself both physically and digitally as things settled into their own neat time line. He would be a few hours yet, trying to cover Torchwood's traces in the matter of Penylan.

Still, his efforts were nothing compared to those of time itself, the ultimate cover-up as people vanished or reappeared, new histories establishing themselves seamlessly over the hundred years or so of Jackson Leaves's influence. Those of them that had been at 'point zero' still had a perfect memory of the night's events –

though he, Gwen and Jack had been working hard since then to alter that fact.

Some things had still played out the same. Joan Bosher had still lived – and died – at Jackson Leaves before bequeathing it to her niece. Rupert Locke's face still stared from the grainy print of old newspapers on his desk as the police took him into custody for his crimes (though there was no mention of where he'd lived), and his statement had become a more honest – if sordid – admission of guilt due to 'his needs'. There were others, though, who had avoided their fates, Kerry Robinson for one. No longer a suicide victim, she had moved to America, and Ianto had tracked her a little as she had worked as a singer for a few years, before family and middle age had tamed her ambition.

At least a few had got away…

Alexander looked up at the cloudy sky and, for the first time since his arrival on the planet, found himself wishing for home. Not that he would be welcome there, of course, but then, the last twenty-four hours had seen him become distinctly unwelcome here, too.

'Mr Martin.' Nurse Sellers was walking across the lawn towards him. 'Perhaps you'd be good enough to tell me why you're getting all this extra attention?'

'What are you talking about, you silly woman?' He wasn't in the mood for her insinuations today.

She bristled at his tone. 'That doctor's here again,' she explained. 'You know, the one from the Council. Says he's got to follow up on a few things. I do hope you haven't got anything *terminal*.'

'Ha!' Alexander laughed to see her drop all pretence of kindness. 'Don't you wish, my dear?' He watched Jack Harkness walking towards him. 'Now bugger off inside while we grown-ups talk business.'

She made an exasperated noise in her throat and stormed off towards the house.

'You do love to make friends,' Jack said as he drew up alongside Alexander.

'It's a skill. I take it this is you firing me from my temporary position?'

'It is.'

Alexander nodded. 'Thought as much. That girly didn't take a liking to me in the end. Can't think why. We got out safely, didn't we?'

'Not all of you.'

'That was always a risk,' Alexander sighed, 'and you know it. Your gallivanting about altering history was far more cavalier and life-threatening, but nobody questions *you*, I notice.'

'You'd be surprised.' Jack began to push Alexander towards the oak tree.

'You'll go too far one day, my boy,' Alexander said. 'And when you do you'd better hope they're more forgiving of you than they were me.'

Jack didn't reply. They stayed in silence beneath the shadow of the tree for a few minutes, each thinking their own thoughts.

'How is that young boy, Joe?' Alexander asked.

'You care?'

'Not particularly,' Alexander admitted.

'He's fine. Had a bit of good fortune, actually. Won a car in a magazine competition.'

'One he doesn't remember entering, I assume?'

'Oh, he remembers it. That and more – doesn't mean any of it happened.'

'Ah… You continue to rewrite history, even now. What are you going to do to me?'

'I don't know,' Jack said softly.

'Yes you do. You just haven't got the balls to do it. You don't know if you can trust me any more, and if you were half the secret soldier you pretend to be you'd act on it. You'd identify me as a problem and take the appropriate action. Given that you can't make me forget – and rest assured you can't; Torchwood may be far more progressed scientifically than the rest of these monkeys, but you're a long way from having sufficient skill to get around my physiognomy – there really is only one way you can solve a problem like me. I'm just interested to know if you're strong enough to carry it out.'

'Maybe I'm not as pragmatic as you,' Jack said, walking away.

'Don't kid yourself,' Alexander called, stretching in his wheelchair and closing his eyes for a doze.

Jack cut across the lawn, avoiding Trudy Topham's waving arms as she pretended to be a butterfly amongst the sparse blooms. There were times when his inability to age or die was a blessing. At least dementia would never get him. Lunacy, perhaps, given his lifestyle, but never dementia.

'Is he ill?' asked a voice from the patio. He looked over to see an elderly man straining over his stout walking cane and glancing between Alexander and Jack.

'Nothing serious,' Jack said, walking over to him. There was something very familiar about the man, but nothing he could place.

'Shame!' the old man chuckled, and the ghosts of twenty Capstans a day rattled around the brittle cage of his chest.

'He doesn't seem to have many friends here,' Jack replied.

'Or anywhere,' the old man agreed. 'Nobody visits him either. Mind you, there's nothing unusual in that. They shove us in here to forget, don't they? Not like in my day. My mother, bless her, lived with us until the day God took her, and I would never have had it any other way…' The old man's voice wavered as he thought about his past. Jack recognised the look only too well, lost in memory…

'I'm sure she appreciated it.'

The old man nodded. 'She did, she did… Poor woman had been abandoned altogether too many times in her life. I certainly wasn't going to add to it.'

'You were a good son.'

Jack smiled, and kept wracking his brain to place the old man. There was definitely something recognisable there, something in his smile… He stuck out his hand. 'Doctor Harkness.'

The old man took it. 'Gordon Cottrell. Pleased to meet you.'

A cold feeling ran through Jack, his skin erupting in gooseflesh. He would have said someone had walked over his grave – he'd certainly had enough of them.

'Cottrell?' he asked. 'What was your mother's name?'

'Alison,' Gordon replied, rather befuddled by the question. 'Why? You're rather young to have known her, I suspect!'

Jack nodded. 'Of course…' He fixed a big, false smile in place. 'Best be off! Patients to see.'

'Aye, well, good talking to you. Maybe see you around again.'

'Maybe.'

Jack had to fight the urge to run as he made his way back towards the car park. He took off his white coat, got back in the SUV and stared out of the windscreen, heart pounding and his breath coming in shallow bursts. After a moment, he pulled a medical tin out of his pocket, opened it, took out the syringe filled with an overdose of anaesthetic he had intended to give Alexander and squirted it out of the window. He put the syringe back in the tin and drove away from Mercy Hill Care Home.

'Hello there,' Gwen said, as Julia opened the door of Jackson Leaves. 'Sorry to disturb you, but I'm from the Council and I just need to ask you a couple of questions.'

Julia checked the identification Gwen was offering and nodded reluctantly once she admitted it all looked in order.

'It's a bit of a mess at the moment,' she said, letting Gwen in and leading her through to the kitchen. 'I still haven't finished unpacking.'

'Never fun, is it?' said Gwen, sitting down at the kitchen table.

'No,' Julia admitted. 'Especially when you're by yourself.'

'Just you then, is it?' Gwen asked. 'Big place for someone on their own.'

'I inherited it from my aunt,' Julia said. 'She rattled around in here for years. I don't think I will.'

'Oh?'

'No… Can't say I like the place much. I'm planning on letting it out. Students, maybe.'

'Oh yes? Why not, eh? Plenty of room.'

'Yeah. I've advertised, but no takers yet. If nobody turns up, I might just sell it, get one of those new apartments at SkyPoint.'

Gwen squirmed. 'I hear they're not all they're cracked up to be.'

'Really?' Julia sighed. 'Just fancied something a bit more modern. Place like this, it's just too…'

'Full of ghosts?' Gwen smiled.

'Something like that.' Julia wiped pointlessly at the kitchen worktop, nervous and wanting something to distract her. 'Well, whatever I decide to do, I need to smarten the place up a bit. Don't suppose you know anyone cheap and reliable, do you? I'm hopeless at that sort of thing. My ex used to do it all, but he's…'

'Yes?'

'Accident at work… I'd rather not go into it.'

'Of course,' Gwen said, getting to her feet. 'I quite understand, and it really is none of my business. Look… This is obviously a bad time. Maybe we can do this over the phone in a couple of weeks?'

'That would be better. Thank you.'

They walked back along the hall to the front door, Gwen stepping outside and smiling as she handed Julia a fake business card. 'I'll call you next month,' she said. 'It's nothing major, just some work we're doing in the area. Oh…' She bent over to pick something up off the gravel. 'Don't leave that lying around. You never know, do you?' She handed the lottery ticket to Julia.

'That's not mine,' Julia said. 'I never do the lottery.'

'Well, it's definitely not mine,' Gwen said. 'I always play the same numbers, my husband's birthday… You may as well hold on to it – never know your luck!'

'I suppose.' Julia didn't seem at all convinced but put the ticket in her pocket anyway.

'Maybe you won't have to worry about finding workmen after all.' Gwen smiled and walked down the drive, waving goodbye over her shoulder.

'Well?' Jack asked as she moved past him and headed for the SUV.

'She's fine. False memory's holding.'

'Good.'

'Excuse me,' came a voice from behind him.

Jack turned to see a young woman jogging towards him.

'Help you?' he asked.

'Hope so!' the girl replied. 'I'm looking for a place that's advertising rooms around here. Nina Rogers…' She stuck out her hand.

'Pleased to meet you, Nina Rogers!' Jack smiled, shaking her hand.

'I'm at the Uni, you wouldn't believe how difficult it is to find somewhere to stay.'

'I can imagine—'

'They're all really expensive or really grotty, or both, I went to this one place, and I swear there were things living in the walls.'

Jack glanced towards Gwen, neither quite sure if they should be worried.

'Like cockroaches or something,' Nina added, her eyes never leaving Jack's face. 'The old guy there probably breeds them, he smelt like the sort, y'know… mouldy… He wore this cardigan that I swear would have stood up on its own, weird guy, wouldn't have stayed there even if the place had been nice, you just can tell about some people, can't you? Not the sort of people you want calling for the rent, if you know what I mean…'

'And breathe…' muttered Gwen with a smile.

'Sorry!' said Nina, rolling her eyes. 'I go on, don't I? Anyway, I've got the advert somewhere…' She dug around in her bag. 'I don't know you, do I?' she said, still looking at Jack.

'Wouldn't be surprised,' Gwen told herself in the SUV's wing mirror.

'I don't think so,' Jack replied with a slight frown.

'He gets around.' Gwen added.

'Here it is!' Nina pulled the advert out. 'Julia Wallace, place called Jackson Leaves.'

'Full, I'm afraid,' Jack said quickly.

'Oh no!' Nina sighed.

'I know. We've actually just come from there. Known the place for years… Hope you find somewhere nice, though.'

Jack headed quickly towards Gwen and the SUV.

'Why did you say that?' Gwen asked. 'You know Julia's looking for tenants.'

'I'm sure the place is OK now, but let's not take the risk. Besides, it's not like Julia will need the money once she cashes in that ticket. It's all worked out just fine, hasn't it?'

Gwen frowned as she glanced at a 'lost' poster on a nearby lamp post – Hannah Ogilvy smiling in an old Christmas photo, paper hat on her head and Christmas-tree earrings that were as jolly as her smile. 'Not for everyone,' she said.

'No,' Jack replied, 'but sometimes you just have to settle for the majority— Watch it!' he shouted as a teenaged boy shoved past him and ran off up the road. 'Wait a minute…' he began checking his pockets.

Gwen was laughing. 'Did you not see who that was?' she asked.

'He took my wallet!'

Jack began to run after him, but Gwen didn't think he stood much of a chance. From what she could see, Danny Wilkinson was a fast runner.

# ACKNOWLEDGEMENTS

Thanks to all the people who had to put up with me while writing this book. My family, who now understand the art of writing: do nothing until the last minute and then type frantically, screaming and begging for the world to end the day before the delivery date. Albert and Nick at BBC Books for keeping a roof over our heads during this process by sending cheques. Steve Tribe not only for giving me the gig in the first place but also for having a name so macho that one cannot help but feel reassured... I picture him as a literary Doug McClure beating primeval creatures to death while correcting my grammar. I hope I never meet him... it's so disheartening to have one's dreams shattered. And, of course, Morris and Pinborough; who'd have thought it, eh?

The rest of you? You're in the book, what more do you want?

# TORCHWOOD
# THE ENCYCLOPEDIA

ISBN 978 1 846 07764 7
£14.99

Founded by Queen Victoria in 1879, the Torchwood Institute has been defending Great Britain from the alien hordes for 130 years. Though London's Torchwood One was destroyed during the Battle of Canary Wharf, the small team at Torchwood Three have continued to monitor the space-time Rift that runs through Cardiff, saving the world and battling for the future of the human race.

Now you can discover every fact and figure, explore every crack in time and encounter every creature that Torchwood have dealt with. Included here are details of:

- The secret of the Children of Earth

- Operatives from Alice Guppy to Gwen Cooper

- Extraterrestrial visitors from Arcateenians to Weevils

- The life and deaths of Captain Jack Harkness

and much more. Illustrated throughout with photos and artwork from all three series, this A–Z provides everything you need to know about Torchwood.

*Based on the hit series created by Russell T Davies for BBC Television.*

# TORCHWOOD
# ANOTHER LIFE
## Peter Anghelides

ISBN 978 0 563 48653 4
£6.99

Thick black clouds are blotting out the skies over Cardiff. As twenty-four inches of rain fall in twenty-four hours, the city centre's drainage system collapses. The capital's homeless are being murdered, their mutilated bodies left lying in the soaked streets around the Blaidd Drwg nuclear facility.

Tracked down by Torchwood, the killer calmly drops eight storeys to his death. But the killings don't stop. Their investigations lead Jack Harkness, Gwen Cooper and Toshiko Sato to a monster in a bathroom, a mystery at an army base and a hunt for stolen nuclear fuel rods. Meanwhile, Owen Harper goes missing from the Hub, when a game in *Second Reality* leads him to an old girlfriend…

Something is coming, forcing its way through the Rift, straight into Cardiff Bay.

*Featuring Captain Jack Harkness as played by John Barrowman, with Gwen Cooper, Owen Harper, Toshiko Sato and Ianto Jones as played by Eve Myles, Burn Gorman, Naoki Mori and Gareth David-Lloyd, in the hit series created by Russell T Davies for BBC Television.*

# TORCHWOOD
# BORDER PRINCES
## Dan Abnett

ISBN 978 0 563 48654 1
£6.99

The End of the World began on a Thursday night in October, just after eight in the evening…

The Amok is driving people out of their minds, turning them into zombies and causing riots in the streets. A solitary diner leaves a Cardiff restaurant, his mission to protect the Principal leading him to a secret base beneath a water tower. Everyone has a headache, there's something in Davey Morgan's shed, and the church of St Mary-in-the-Dust, demolished in 1840, has reappeared – though it's not due until 2011. Torchwood seem to be out of their depth. What will all this mean for the romance between Torchwood's newest members?

Captain Jack Harkness has something more to worry about: an alarm, an early warning, given to mankind and held – inert – by Torchwood for 108 years. And now it's flashing. Something is coming. Or something is already here.

*Featuring Captain Jack Harkness as played by John Barrowman, with Gwen Cooper, Owen Harper, Toshiko Sato and Ianto Jones as played by Eve Myles, Burn Gorman, Naoki Mori and Gareth David-Lloyd, in the hit series created by Russell T Davies for BBC Television.*

*Also available from BBC Books*

T O R C H W O O D
# SLOW DECAY
## Andy Lane

ISBN 978 0 563 48655 8
£6.99

When Torchwood track an energy surge to a Cardiff nightclub, the team finds the police are already at the scene. Five teenagers have died in a fight, and lying among the bodies is an unfamiliar device. Next morning, they discover the corpse of a Weevil, its face and neck eaten away, seemingly by human teeth. And on the streets of Cardiff, an ordinary woman with an extraordinary hunger is attacking people and eating her victims.

The job of a lifetime it might be, but working for Torchwood is putting big strains on Gwen's relationship with Rhys. While she decides to spice up their love life with the help of alien technology, Rhys decides it's time to sort himself out – better music, healthier food, lose some weight. Luckily, a friend has mentioned Doctor Scotus's weight-loss clinic…

*Featuring Captain Jack Harkness as played by John Barrowman, with Gwen Cooper, Owen Harper, Toshiko Sato and Ianto Jones as played by Eve Myles, Burn Gorman, Naoki Mori and Gareth David-Lloyd, in the hit series created by Russell T Davies for BBC Television.*

*Also available from BBC Books*

T O R C H W O O D
# SOMETHING IN THE WATER
## Trevor Baxendale

ISBN 978 1 84607 437 0
£6.99

Dr Bob Strong's GP surgery has been treating a lot of coughs and colds recently, far more than is normal for the time of year. Bob thinks there's something up but he can't think what. He seems to have caught it himself, whatever it is – he's starting to cough badly and there are flecks of blood in his hanky.

Saskia Harden has been found on a number of occasions submerged in ponds or canals but alive and seemingly none the worse for wear. Saskia is not on any files, except in the medical records at Dr Strong's GP practice.

But Torchwood's priorities lie elsewhere: investigating ghostly apparitions in South Wales, they have found a dead body. It's old and in an advanced state of decay. And it is still able to talk.

And what it is saying is 'Water hag'…

*Featuring Captain Jack Harkness as played by John Barrowman, with Gwen Cooper, Owen Harper, Toshiko Sato and Ianto Jones as played by Eve Myles, Burn Gorman, Naoki Mori and Gareth David-Lloyd, in the hit series created by Russell T Davies for BBC Television.*

TORCHWOOD
# TRACE MEMORY
## David Llewellyn

ISBN 978 1 84607 438 7
£6.99

Tiger Bay, Cardiff, 1953. A mysterious crate is brought into the docks on a Scandinavian cargo ship. Its destination: the Torchwood Institute. As the crate is offloaded by a group of local dockers, it explodes, killing all but one of them, a young Butetown lad called Michael Bellini.

Fifty-five years later, a radioactive source somewhere inside the Hub leads Torchwood to discover the same Michael Bellini, still young and dressed in his 1950s clothes, cowering in the vaults. They soon realise that each has encountered Michael before – as a child in Osaka, as a junior doctor, as a young police constable, as a new recruit to Torchwood One. But it's Jack who remembers him best of all.

Michael's involuntary time-travelling has something to do with a radiation-charged relic held inside the crate. And the Men in Bowler Hats are coming to get it back.

*Featuring Captain Jack Harkness as played by John Barrowman, with Gwen Cooper, Owen Harper, Toshiko Sato and Ianto Jones as played by Eve Myles, Burn Gorman, Naoki Mori and Gareth David-Lloyd, in the hit series created by Russell T Davies for BBC Television.*

*Also available from BBC Books*

TORCHWOOD
# THE TWILIGHT STREETS
## Gary Russell

ISBN 978 1 846 07439 4
£6.99

There's a part of the city that no one much goes to, a collection of rundown old houses and gloomy streets. No one stays there long, and no one can explain why – something's not quite right there.

Now the Council is renovating the district, and a new company is overseeing the work. There will be street parties and events to show off the newly gentrified neighbourhood: clowns and face-painters for the kids, magicians for the adults – the street entertainers of Cardiff, out in force.

None of this is Torchwood's problem. Until Toshiko recognises the sponsor of the street parties: Bilis Manger.

Now there is something for Torchwood to investigate. But Captain Jack Harkness has never been able to get into the area; it makes him physically ill to go near it. Without Jack's help, Torchwood must face the darker side of urban Cardiff alone…

*Featuring Captain Jack Harkness as played by John Barrowman, with Gwen Cooper, Owen Harper, Toshiko Sato and Ianto Jones as played by Eve Myles, Burn Gorman, Naoki Mori and Gareth David-Lloyd, in the hit series created by Russell T Davies for BBC Television.*

*Also available from BBC Books*

TORCHWOOD
# PACK ANIMALS
## Peter Anghelides

ISBN 978 1 846 07574 2
£6.99

Shopping for wedding gifts is enjoyable, unless like Gwen you witness a Weevil massacre in the shopping centre. A trip to the zoo is a great day out, until a date goes tragically wrong and Ianto is badly injured by stolen alien tech. And Halloween is a day of fun and frights, before unspeakable monsters invade the streets of Cardiff and it's no longer a trick or a treat for the terrified population.

Torchwood can control small groups of scavengers, but now someone has given large numbers of predators a season ticket to Earth. Jack's investigation is hampered when he finds he's being investigated himself. Owen is convinced that it's just one guy who's toying with them. But will Torchwood find out before it's too late that the game is horribly real, and the deck is stacked against them?

*Featuring Captain Jack Harkness as played by John Barrowman, with Gwen Cooper, Owen Harper, Toshiko Sato and Ianto Jones as played by Eve Myles, Burn Gorman, Naoki Mori and Gareth David-Lloyd, in the hit series created by Russell T Davies for BBC Television.*

'If you're going to be anyone in Cardiff, you're going to be at SkyPoint!'

SkyPoint is the latest high-rise addition to the ever-developing Cardiff skyline. It's the most high-tech, avant-garde apartment block in the city. And it's where Rhys Williams is hoping to find a new home for himself and Gwen. Gwen's more concerned by the money behind the tower block – Besnik Lucca, a name she knows from her days in uniform.

When Torchwood discover that residents have been going missing from the tower block, one of the team gets her dream assignment. Soon SkyPoint's latest newly married tenants are moving in. And Toshiko Sato finally gets to make a home with Owen Harper.

Then something comes out of the wall…

*Featuring Captain Jack Harkness as played by John Barrowman, with Gwen Cooper, Owen Harper, Toshiko Sato and Ianto Jones as played by Eve Myles, Burn Gorman, Naoki Mori and Gareth David-Lloyd, in the hit series created by Russell T Davies for BBC Television.*

*Also available from BBC Books*

# TORCHWOOD
# ALMOST PERFECT
## James Goss

ISBN 978 1 846 07573 5
£6.99

Emma is 30, single and frankly desperate. She woke up this morning with nothing to look forward to but another evening of unsuccessful speed-dating. But now she has a new weapon in her quest for Mr Right. And it's made her almost perfect.

Gwen Cooper woke up this morning expecting the unexpected. As usual. She went to work and found a skeleton at a table for two and a colleague in a surprisingly glamorous dress. Perfect.

Ianto Jones woke up this morning with no memory of last night. He went to work, where he caused amusement, suspicion and a little bit of jealousy. Because Ianto Jones woke up this morning in the body of a woman. And he's looking just about perfect.

Jack Harkness has always had his doubts about Perfection.

*Featuring Captain Jack Harkness as played by John Barrowman, with Gwen Cooper and Ianto Jones as played by Eve Myles and Gareth David-Lloyd, in the hit series created by Russell T Davies for BBC Television.*

# TORCHWOOD
# INTO THE SILENCE
## Sarah Pinborough

ISBN 978 1 846 07753 1
£6.99

The body in the church hall is very definitely dead. It has been sliced open with surgical precision, its organs exposed, and its vocal cords are gone. It is as if they were never there or they've been dissolved…

With the Welsh Amateur Operatic Contest getting under way, music is filling the churches and concert halls of Cardiff. The competition has attracted the finest Welsh talent to the city, but it has also drawn something else – there are stories of a metallic creature hiding in the shadows. Torchwood are on its tail, but it's moving too fast for them to track it down.

This new threat requires a new tactic – so Ianto Jones is joining a male voice choir…

*Featuring Captain Jack Harkness as played by John Barrowman, with Gwen Cooper and Ianto Jones as played by Eve Myles and Gareth David-Lloyd, in the hit series created by Russell T Davies for BBC Television.*

**Also available from BBC Books**

T O R C H W O O D
# BAY OF THE DEAD
## Mark Morris

ISBN 978 1 846 07737 1
£6.99

When the city sleeps, the dead start to walk…

Something has sealed off Cardiff, and living corpses are stalking the streets, leaving a trail of half-eaten bodies. Animals are butchered. A young couple in their car never reach their home. A stolen yacht is brought back to shore, carrying only human remains. And a couple of girls heading back from the pub watch the mysterious drivers of a big black SUV take over a crime scene.

Torchwood have to deal with the intangible barrier surrounding Cardiff, and some unidentified space debris that seems to be regenerating itself. Plus, of course, the all-night zombie horror show.

Not that they really believe in zombies.

*Featuring Captain Jack Harkness as played by John Barrowman, with Gwen Cooper and Ianto Jones as played by Eve Myles and Gareth David-Lloyd, in the hit series created by Russell T Davies for BBC Television.*

*Coming soon from BBC Books*

T O R C H W O O D
# THE UNDERTAKER'S GIFT
## Trevor Baxendale

ISBN 978 1 846 07782 1
£6.99

The Hokrala Corp lawyers are back. They're suing planet Earth for mishandling the twenty-first century, and they won't tolerate any efforts to repel them. An assassin has been sent to remove Captain Jack Harkness.

It's been a busy week in Cardiff. The Hub's latest guest is a translucent, amber jelly carrying a lethal electrical charge. Record numbers of aliens have been coming through the Rift, and Torchwood could do without any more problems.

But there are reports of an extraordinary funeral cortege in the night-time city, with mysterious pallbearers guarding a rotting cadaver that simply doesn't want to be buried.

Torchwood should be ready for anything – but with Jack the target of an invisible killer, Gwen trapped in a forgotten crypt and Ianto Jones falling desperately ill, could a world of suffering be the Undertaker's gift to planet Earth?

*Featuring Captain Jack Harkness as played by John Barrowman, with Gwen Cooper and Ianto Jones as played by Eve Myles and Gareth David-Lloyd, in the hit series created by Russell T Davies for BBC Television.*

# TORCHWOOD
# RISK ASSESSMENT
## James Goss

ISBN 978 1 846 07783 8
£6.99

'Are you trying to tell me, Captain Harkness, that the entire staff of Torchwood Cardiff now consists of yourself, a woman in trousers and a tea boy?'

Agnes Haversham is awake, and Jack is worried (and not a little afraid). The Torchwood Assessor is roused from her deep sleep in only the worst of times – it's happened just four times in the last 100 years. Can the situation really be so bad?

Someone, somewhere, is fighting a war, and they're losing badly. The coffins of the dead are coming through the Rift. With thousands of alien bodies floating in the Bristol Channel, it's down to Torchwood to round them all up before a lethal plague breaks out.

And now they'll have to do it by the book. The 1901 edition.

*Featuring Captain Jack Harkness as played by John Barrowman, with Gwen Cooper and Ianto Jones as played by Eve Myles and Gareth David-Lloyd, in the hit series created by Russell T Davies for BBC Television.*

# TORCHWOOD
# CONSEQUENCES

ISBN 978 1 846 07784 5
£6.99

Saving the planet, watching over the Rift, preparing the human race for the twenty-first century... Torchwood has been keeping Cardiff safe since the late 1800s. Small teams of heroes, working 24/7, encountering and containing the alien, the bizarre and the inexplicable.

But Torchwood do not always see the effects of their actions. What links the Rules and Regulations for replacing a Torchwood leader to the destruction of a shopping centre? How does a witness to an alien's reprisals against Torchwood become caught up in a night of terror in a university library? And why should Gwen and Ianto's actions at a local publishers have a cost for Torchwood more than half a century earlier?

For Torchwood, the past will always catch up with them. And sometimes the future will catch up with the past...

*Featuring stories by writers for the hit series created by Russell T Davies for BBC Television, including Joseph Lidster and James Moran, plus Andrew Cartmel, David Llewellyn and Sarah Pinborough.*